Enlightened

Allyson Richards

AuthorHouse™
1663 Liberty Drive
Bloomington, IN 47403
www.authorhouse.com
Phone: 1-800-839-8640

First published by AuthorHouse 2/22/2011

ISBN: 978-1-4567-2257-9 (sc)
ISBN: 978-1-4567-2258-6 (e)

Library of Congress Control Number: 2010919578

Printed in the United States of America

To mom, who made my craziest dream come true.

Prologue

I was walking down a familiar sidewalk, the one with trees lining either side, where the sun always seemed to shine, and that always seemed too perfect for my world. I took this path every day on my way home from school.

I hated my school. I truly and utterly HATED my school. I must have told my mom a hundred times a day that I didn't belong there. I didn't belong in any school—period. What could someone like me get out of school?

I guess sitting in class and walking through the halls was good practice for controlling my anger, but it was way too risky for me to be that close to regular people—or "Normals," as I like to call them—for long periods of time. I had begged my mom to homeschool me, but she always said that I'd be happier in school and around people my own age instead of isolating myself.

HA! I did that anyway! Did she really think I had anything to do with Normals, even in school? NO WAY! I kept as far away from them as possible. I didn't even talk to the kids at my school, let alone hang out with them! People there didn't seem to notice me, and if they did, they certainly didn't make an effort to get to know me. I liked to keep it that way.

I knew that if I got too cozy around Normals, I would forget how fragile they are to me, and if I were to lose control—get too angry—and they were too close to me, I might.... I couldn't even finish that thought. It never failed to send a shiver of fear down my spine.

The faint sound of a loud, obnoxious car slowly brought me back to reality. The sound seemed to be coming from behind me—and was getting closer. In a minute, a red Mustang convertible pulled alongside me, revving its engine.

Of course, it was none other than the awful, nauseating, repellent Cindy Wafer.

She was the prettiest and most popular girl in my entire high school. She was a sophomore, like me, and was determined to make my life miserable—which wasn't too hard, seeing as it wasn't all that great to begin with.

"Hey, chatty Kathy!" she called from her car.

Ha. Ha. Chatty Kathy... because I don't talk to anyone... she's so freaking clever.

Just an FYI, my name is actually Alexis.

I rolled my eyes and avoided hers.

"You need a lift?" she asked.

I kept walking, trying to breathe evenly.

"Come on, aren't those old, worn sneakers killing your poor little feet?"

She really wasn't making this easy for me.

"I won't bite," Cindy said with a smirk.

Maybe she wouldn't, but I knew I could do a lot worse to her.

"All right, be that way. But before I go, you look like you're kind of hot... I'll take care of that."

She hit the gas pedal and ran through a puddle on the side of the road, spraying me with dirty leftover rainwater.

I stood still for a moment, shocked at what Cindy had done. A second later, my arms and legs started to go numb. Adrenaline pulsed hot through my veins as my hands curled into violent fists.

I managed to control my anger until Cindy's convertible was out of sight and I could destroy something. Without thinking, I yelled and kicked a fire hydrant on the sidewalk. With one swing of my leg, the hydrant went flying, and water spewed immediately from the ground. Now instead of a girl with a few splatters on her pants, I looked like I had taken a shower with all of my clothes on. Yeah, that was much better.

As my anger subsided, I realized that I needed to haul you-know-what back home before someone saw me. I began jogging down the sidewalk in the direction of the forest. Once I got under the cover of the trees, I could run at full speed. I would be home—and somewhat dry—in less than a minute or so if I ran fast enough.

I pretty much beat myself up most of the way, but what I was really worried about was what Mom would have to say once she found out what I did *this* time.

Chapter 1

"In other news, a mysterious flooding has occurred on Maple Street. The entire north end has been shut down to prevent accidents, so if you were planning on taking that route, you might need to find an alternative. According to city sources, the flood has been caused by a missing fire hydrant."

When I heard the news anchor say "missing fire hydrant," I snickered like a little kid enjoying his own practical joke.

"The hydrant itself has not been found, and the surrounding area shows no signs of a car accident that might have dislodged it from its base. Authorities are baffled and cannot offer any logical explanation for the absence of this hydrant."

Boy, did Mom chew me a new one for that little stunt.

Honestly, I shouldn't have been surprised that I got caught, given that my mother could read minds.

It wasn't Mom's fault that I was an uncontrollable weapon of mass destruction. I couldn't have inherited this unique characteristic from her since Mom and I are completely different.

She has the ability to read people's thoughts, feelings, emotions, dreams, and even their fears. She can do other cool psychological things, too, like "mind-wiping" people so they forget everything they've just seen. But her abilities are more like a talent compared to the curse that was thrust upon me.

What I have—it sounds so stupid to even say it—is superhuman strength and speed. That's right, I'm like a freakish girl superhero. I can run amazingly fast—a couple of hundred miles in an hour or so—and I can pick up stuff like trees and cars. Unfortunately, my powers are mostly destructive. When I get mad, I can tear down a house, throw things a couple miles, or even rip you to pieces if I really wanted to.

My grandparents have powers, too, I think. My mom and I have never really talked about our family. That probably has to do with the fact that most of my relatives are kind of messed up. Dad ditched us when I was barely able to talk, and my grandpa has had one foot on a banana peel and the other in the loony bin for years now. But in the midst of all that crap, my mom and grandma are the best a bizarre, super-powered girl could ask for. I'm pretty sure I have a couple of great aunts, but my mom's an only child, so other than that, no aunts, uncles, or cousins… unless good ol' dad had any siblings.

I have no idea who my mysterious father is or even if he's still alive.

But if he's anything like me, I don't think I'd like to meet him. Maybe somehow I inherited this awful nuisance from him.

Speaking of awful nuisance… just thinking about my dad made the power flow through my veins. Huh… I hadn't realized I was getting irritated. Oh well, it was nothing I couldn't handle. I didn't really know how the curse worked, but the one thing I knew for sure was that if I didn't control my negative emotions, things tended to get ugly.

On the day after the incident with the fire hydrant, I was back on the same sidewalk, heading home from school. I wasn't paying attention to where I was walking (that could have had to do with the earphones that were blasting music into my eardrums) until I bumped into someone by accident.

"Ouch. Oops. Watch it," a slightly deep voice said.

I really didn't appreciate the way he was talking to me. *Oh, he's gonna be sorry.*

"Excuse me?" I said in a stiff, edgy tone. But that was before I got a good look at his face. I'm not going to lie to you. I was shocked at what I saw.

At first when I looked up, I saw nothing but a big, broad chest with a dark shirt covering it. Then, I adjusted my gaze upward and found myself looking at a perfect face. He had shaggy black hair that was brushed across his forehead, revealing his dark—almost black—

mysterious eyes. I couldn't tell exactly what color they were; I just knew that they looked mystifying and deep.

I'm sure my eyes were almost popping out of my head and my mouth was hanging open; I must have looked like an idiot. I tried to erase the shock from my face and take in his expression. His face seemed hard and rigid, but his eyes revealed a hint of admiration. And a bit of uneasiness.

For about three seconds, he stood on the sidewalk, motionless, almost frozen in place. Then, a grin stretched across his face. His smile was warm and friendly and… pleased? *Huh, I wonder what he's thinking.* Before I could come up with an answer for myself, he opened his mouth to speak.

"Hi, there," he said in an angelically smooth voice. It goes against everything I believe in, but how could I NOT talk to a face that amazing?

"Hi," I said in a more cheerful tone. That was all I could come up with. I tried to flash him my best smile, but it was clear that I couldn't do any better than a nervous smirk. I could feel the awkward contortion of my face, and I felt a little self-conscious about it.

When he saw my pathetic excuse for a smile, his widened into the biggest, whitest, most perfect example I had ever seen in my life. His teeth were so white that they literally made his dark features gleam.

We stood on the sidewalk, gazing at each other for what felt like hours (but I think it was only about five or six seconds) before he spoke up.

"Oh, umm… I'm Taylor."

It took me a second to sort out my thoughts before I finally spoke. "Alexis," I managed to reply. Inside, my mind and heart were at war. It was as if my mind was screaming logic and common sense into my eardrums, while my heart was gently nudging me toward Taylor. I could feel my heart winning.

"Well, nice to meet you, Alexis," he said as he held out his big, strong hand. I stared at his hand, patiently waiting to take mine, while an inner debate raged.

My heart was telling me, "Just shake it, and don't be rude!" while my mind fired back, "Yeah, and you know what else is rude? Crushing the guy's hand!" That was the kind of logic that my heart couldn't argue with.

After a moment, Taylor pulled his hand away and started rubbing the back and side of his neck. I'd seen people do this when they were nervous or anxious, but why was he nervous around me all of a sudden? *Does he not like me?* I wasn't scary looking on the outside. I looked just like any other sixteen-year-old girl. Of course, the inside was a whole different story. Suddenly, I snapped back to reality.

This was exactly what I'd always wanted from Normals—to stay away from me before they learned what I was really like. So why was I still standing here with Taylor, worrying about why he might be nervous or anxious? Why did I care if he liked me or not?

I felt my hands starting to tremble and ball up into fists. Oh no. I was getting anxious. This situation was going to get bad quickly if I didn't get away—fast. UGH! I knew it was a mistake to stop!

I turned around and started running away from Taylor at half speed. I couldn't go full speed because that would give my secret away right then and there. But for me, jogging was more than enough to get me away from Taylor before he got hurt. I heard him yell from behind me.

"Wait!" But I couldn't wait, even though part of me wished that I could.

Great, now he really doesn't like me. Maybe I should turn around and apologize. At least I could've said goodbye to him before I took off like a freaking maniac! I suddenly realized exactly what I was thinking… and snapped. I automatically burst into lightning speed and veered into the woods so that no one could see me… or get killed because they got in my way.

After just a few seconds, I was several miles away from Taylor and the sidewalk. I knew this because there were a lot of trees in this area that looked as if they'd been lifted straight up from the ground, roots and all, and snapped like twigs, right in half.

This spot was where I came when I needed to vent my anger. You know how some people tell kids to beat up a pillow when they get mad? When I was little, my mom had taught me to beat up a tree. It probably wasn't very environmentally conscious, but it kept me from hurting other people. Now when I felt myself losing control, I'd run out to the mountains near our home and take out my rage on a couple of nice thick oaks. Sometimes a mountain lion would stop by to be slaughtered because he came to the wrong place at the wrong time. On the day I met Taylor, though, I just plopped onto the rocky soil and let out a big huff of breath.

Wow. That's something new.

Not that I wasn't happy that I didn't have to crush a mountain lion or snap some trees to calm myself down. I usually have this indescribable, overwhelming desire to destroy anything that makes me angry. On that day, I was calm.

Had I finally learned to control my powers?

I laughed at the thought. My curse had been part of me ever since I could remember. Still, my reaction was weird.

A lot of things in my life remained a mystery, though, so I decided not to worry too much about this sudden shift in my emotions. Since I was calm, I shrugged my shoulders and headed back to my house. Mom was probably having a panic attack. It would take only a few seconds to get to the house if I ran at full speed, but I kind of wanted to enjoy a nice walk through the forest.

Not only did I have a sense of calm, but I felt at peace. For once, I was in control of all my thoughts and feelings. I can't really describe the sensation; for me, it was like finding a whole new kind of happiness. I wasn't familiar with this kind of emotion, but I really liked it. Somehow, it felt like stepping outside on one of those cool, crisp autumn days, when there's not a cloud in the sky and lots of sunshine, when it seems like all your problems could be puffed away by a refreshingly light breeze.

The forest definitely seemed to be in a better mood, as well. The thinner trees swayed lightly in the breeze, while the stronger ones stood tall and proud, their leaves ruffling softly. I saw cardinals and blue jays sitting high in a beautiful oak tree and squirrels chasing each other playfully. It sounds a little silly to say it, but I was intoxicated by the beauty around me.

Ten or fifteen minutes passed during my walk through the woods before I arrived home. I knew I was late, and I was one hundred percent sure I was going to hear it from my mom. Knowing that my sense of tranquility was about to disappear, I took a deep breath before opening the front door.

The hinges creaked loudly as I entered the front of my house. The smell of dinner filled my nose the second I walked into the hallway. I hadn't realized how hungry I was, but once I thought about it, dinner seemed like a wonderful idea. I heard my stomach growl in agreement.

A short hallway led to the living room, which was tidy and spare. All that sat here were two medium-sized couches, an easy chair, and a large coffee table in the middle. To the right was the kitchen. Mom was in there cooking, just as I had figured.

My mom is not much taller than I am. She's about five foot, five, so I'm not too far behind her. She looks like me except a little older; she could easily be mistaken for my older sister. No joke, she looks like she's in her early twenties. She has really long, light blonde hair and bright blue eyes to match. Not only does she look like she's twenty, but she acts like it, too. A lot of the time, I consider her a best friend. But something in my head told me that this wouldn't be one of those times.

Luckily, the stove faces the rear of the house, so my mom's back was toward me when I entered the kitchen.

Was there any possibility that she hadn't noticed my absence and that I could sneak by without getting caught?

"Nice try, but I noticed," my mother answered. "You know better than that." Her tone wasn't furious, as I had anticipated, not even the least bit angry, which kind of threw me off.

"Hey, Mom, sorry, I know I'm late, but I can explain..." I was trying to come up with something, but my mom cut me off.

"That's okay, I understand. It's no big deal. So how was school?"

Mom sounded way too understanding. Way too happy, come to think of it.

"Good...," I said in a hesitant, cautious voice.

"No homework?" she asked.

"Okay, Mom, what's going on? Where are you trying to go with this motherly act?" I was starting to get irritated because she was definitely up to something.

"What do you mean?" she asked in an angelic tone.

"You just seem... I don't know, like you're trying to...." My sentence trailed off because I forgot what I was going to say. That's another one of Mom's annoying talents; she can scramble your thoughts. It lasts only a couple minutes, but you forget what you were doing or talking about.

Mom turned around for the first time in the whole conversation. I could tell she was smiling when her back was to me, and I could hear a hint of laughter in her voice.

"Okay, then, dinner will be ready in ten minutes. I'm making spaghetti. Are you hungry?" There was a pause before I spoke. I was still pulling my thoughts together.

"Umm, yeah, I am, sounds great. I'm just going to go change." I started to walk away, but my mom stopped me as I was halfway out the kitchen door.

"Oh, Alexis, one more thing." Crap, I knew she was trying to weasel something out of me.

"Yes?" I asked impatiently.

"Why were you so late coming home from school? Did something happen?" She didn't sound too concerned, so I figured she was just trying to make pleasant conversation.

I thought I had managed to sneak one by her and could get away clean. Now, I felt guilty.

"Oh… that? It was nothing. I… I just decided to take a walk through the forest on my way home." That didn't sound too convincing. Did she notice?

"Oh, okay, then. Just wondering." I turned to leave the kitchen again, but she said, "So… did you meet anyone *new* today? Possibly outside of school… like a boy?" Her smile was a little too smug for my liking. Then, I realized that she knew.

"MOM!" I cried out furiously, "How could you?!"

"How could I what?" she asked.

"Look in my mind! You totally invaded my privacy! How could you lead me on like that?" I was dangerously angry now, but because my mom has her "psychological talents," she knows how to calm my emotions so that I can't hurt her.

"Well, honey," she started to explain, "it's very hard *not* to read your thoughts when you're practically screaming a boy's name in your head. And when a boy's name came up… well, I couldn't resist seeing what this Taylor fellow looked like." She had a crooked grin perched on her face. I felt both shocked and violated. My mother reads my mind all the time, but she never *looks* inside my head. I was surprised at her.

"So..." she began.

"So, what?" I asked, still angry.

"Is he nice?" Her eyes brightened with enthusiasm, and her crooked grin turned into an excited smile.

"I guess so," I said in a rude tone.

"How old is he?" she asked again. I was starting to get irritated.

"Sixteen or seventeen, maybe. I don't know."

"So what school does..." I cut her off in mid-sentence.

"MOM, Do you honestly think I know every detail of this stranger's life? We didn't even talk, OKAY? I just bumped into him; we both said sorry; I started to lose control, so I took a walk; and now, I'm here. Is THAT enough detail?!" I was trying to catch my breath after my outburst when I noticed that my mom's eyes were wide with disbelief. I realized I might have hurt her feelings.

"Look, Mom, I'm sor—" She held a hand up to cut me off. She had her eyes closed and her eyebrows pulled together as if she was thinking hard.

"Back up a minute, Lex. What did you say?" Now, she was confusing me.

"What do you mean?" I asked tensely.

"Repeat what you said after the part about starting to lose control."

I wasn't sure what she was trying to make of all of this, but her eyes were open now, staring at me intently. She was waiting for my answer, and she was growing impatient.

"Um, well…, like I said, I started to lose it, so I ran to the woods…."

Mom tried to finish my sentence for me: "…where you went completely insane and started snapping trees in half, right?" She had only seen me out of control in the forest a couple of times, but I knew that each time it happened, she was completely mortified.

Who could blame her?

"Actually, no. I thought I was going to go ballistic, but once I stopped running, all the power washed away. It was pretty amazing." I could feel a smile creeping up on me now. I remembered the feeling of tranquility, control, and something else that I still couldn't put my finger on. All I could say was that it felt great.

"Wait a minute, are you sure you were about to lose control?"

"Positive. I felt the power growing inside me when I was running, but once I was in the clearing, it just… stopped." My mother seemed just as confused as I was.

"Hmm… this is very strange. Not that I'm not thrilled to hear that you controlled yourself, but it doesn't make sense…." She let her sentence trail off as she started thinking again.

"Oh… Mom. I know what you're thinking, but don't fuss too much about it. It was probably just a spur-of-the-moment thing, you know? I know for a fact that I'm long, long way from ever figuring out my curse, so let's just drop it, okay?" My mother clenched her jaw and gave me a disapproving look, the one she always gives me when I refer to my "powers" as a curse (which they are).

"Lex, when are you going to realize that you do not have a curse and that you have much more to offer the world than you think you do?"

"Never. Because I do have a curse and I don't have anything good to offer the world. I'm a threat and a danger. End of story, no questions asked." I really wasn't in the mood for this debate… again. Mom and I must go through it at least twice a week.

"No, that's *not* the end of the story." She was getting irritated, too. Her voice became firm and fierce. "You don't realize that this 'curse' is really a talent. Why is it so hard for you to see your true potential? Why do you drown in your own self-pity?!" I was getting extremely angry now, but my mother still had a hold on my emotions.

My eyes were squeezed shut as I fought back tears. I rubbed the bridge of my nose with my thumb and index finger, trying to stay calm enough to talk to my mother. Obviously, it didn't work.

"Self-pity! Are you KIDDING ME?! I have never heard anything more uncalled for in my life!!! You just don't get it, do you?!"

"Apparently, I don't!"

"I DON'T FEEL SORRY FOR MYSELF! I FEEL TERRIFIED

OF MYSELF... AND SCARED FOR THE PEOPLE AROUND ME!!!" Tears trickled down my face. I took a deep breath and continued in a more measured tone: "Mom, one false move and it's all over: an innocent person's life, our secret, and our lives. You have no idea what a monster I feel like." Wow. In all the arguments I'd had with my mother, I'd never told her that. I don't know what came over me, but all my emotions just... exploded.

"Oh, Alexis..." She came around the counter and hugged me.

With my mom's arms around me, my trickling tears turned into a waterfall. I don't think I'd ever cried so hard.

"Honey, please listen to me." Mom's tone was calm and soothing now. "You are not by any means a monster. You are an amazing girl, and once you get over your fear of being around people, I know you're going to do great things." My tears had slowed down a bit now and my whimpering had passed.

"Thanks for believing in me, Mom, but don't get your hopes up." I gave her a final squeeze and backed away. "I'm going to go change out of my school clothes."

Mom still had a serious look on her face, but now, she seemed more worried than disapproving.

"Okay, Lex, dinner will be ready soon." I nodded and turned away, starting down the hall to my room.

Usually, after my mom and I have our little debate about how I can offer more to the world (blah, blah, blah) and I try to clarify the fact that I have no business being around people (blah, blah, blah), we both move on. But something told me that my mother wasn't willing to give up this argument. Not after I had told her how I really felt and *definitely* not after I had told her about my little scene in the clearing. Nope, she wouldn't drop the subject that easily this time.

Chapter 2

The weather was perfectly pleasant as I made my way home—the sky clear, the sun bright and warm but not hot. The brisk air put me in an unusually good mood, especially given that I had just gotten out of school.

To my astonishment, the day hadn't been half bad. None of the Normals had given me a reason to get irritated with them, and I'd happily maintained my low profile. For once, life had decided to give me a break.

"Hey, Alexis?" a voice called from behind me.

Crap. I spoke too soon.

I swallowed hard as my heart thudded heavily. I thought I recognized the voice, but I was scared to turn around and have my intuition confirmed.

Yep, it was Taylor.

"Alexis, wait up!" he said as he jogged toward me.

Oh my Gosh. Oh my Gosh. What should I do? What should I do?

The way I saw it, I had two simple options: Stay or skedaddle. My brain told me to run, but my heart told me to stay. Guess which one I picked.

"Hi, Taylor," I said nervously as he finally caught up to me. I'm always amazed at how slow Normals are.

He smiled as he brushed his hair away from his eyes. He was wearing a black leather jacket over a T-shirt with some band's name on it and a pair of dark jeans.

Oh, GREAT—he's even hotter than he was yesterday!

"So," he began, catching his breath, "what happened to you yesterday?" I looked away in embarrassment, remembering how I'd taken off with no explanation.

"Sorry, I— I was late getting home again," I stammered.

"Ah, parents are strict, huh?" he asked casually.

"Not really; my mom's pretty cool. She just worries a lot," I said, more comfortably this time.

I knew I shouldn't get this close to a Normal, but I couldn't help myself. I mean, you should have seen this boy!

"I wish my parents were around to worry," Taylor said, his voice sounding stiff.

"What are they, like, deadbeats?" I asked bluntly.

"Actually, just dead," he responded.

Way to go Alexis.

"Oh, I— I'm sorry," I began, trying to recover, but Taylor stopped me.

"It's okay; they died when I was little. I don't really remember them all that well."

"Still, it's got to be hard," I said, feeling terrible—both for what I'd said and for him. He shrugged as we walked down the sidewalk. After an awkward silence, Taylor spoke again.

"What are your 'rents like?"

I shrugged. "Like I said, my mom's pretty cool. She works a lot as a nurse, but since I'm an only child, she finds time for me."

"What about your dad?" he asked. His words stung, as if he had slapped me across the face.

"M.I.A.," I replied, trying to keep my voice level.

"When did he leave?" Taylor asked, suddenly enthralled by my family situation.

My hands shook and my shoulders tensed. Usually, I would take off running before my anger grew worse, but now, I tried to push the emotions aside and answered.

"Why does it matter?" I spat. He got the hint that dear old dad was a sore subject and dropped it.

We had strayed from my usual route home from school and ended up at a small park about a quarter of a mile away from my house.

There wasn't much to it—a jungle gym filled with kids, a sitting area nearby for the parents, and a little pond about twenty yards away from the land of munchkins. It was a cute fish pond, home to some pretty water lilies and a family of ducks.

Taylor and I sat together near the edge of the water.

"Have you lived in Tennessee long?" he asked as he picked up a small rock and tossed it into the water.

"Yeah, seven years or so. We moved here when I was in second grade," I answered, watching as his rock skipped twice before sinking into the murky water.

"Where did you live before?" he asked as he leaned back on his elbows to keep himself upright.

I wasn't too sure why he was asking all these questions. He could have been making pleasant conversation, but being my paranoid self, I was sure he must have had a motive. I tried to find something in his expression, but he seemed to be able to hide his emotions—if he was feeling any at all. He was mysterious looking. I almost…liked it.

"Up in northeast Virginia."

"What made you come here?"

I almost laughed out loud when I remembered the day we had to move.

It had been a beautiful day—much like this one—and I'd heard the ice cream man's truck coming through our neighborhood. I got the money from my mom and went outside to wait for him. I waited patiently on the sidewalk, but the truck passed me by. I got so mad that I ran after the truck and singlehandedly tipped it over. That's also the story of how I discovered my curse. For such a deadly ability, it's a pretty cute story.

"Mom got a better opportunity at the hospital here, so we moved," I lied. Taylor nodded as he watched me pick up a flat stone and launch it halfway across the pond, scattering the family of ducks.

He let out a long whistle and said, "Six skips? Impressive."

I was fully aware that if I lost my self-control for any reason, Taylor could get seriously hurt, but I was still glad that I'd run into him. Why I was so comfortable around him, I might never know. But I did know that there was something special about him. And not just because I thought he was the most gorgeous guy I had ever met in my life. There was something about Taylor that made me feel… *connected* to him.

I smiled at him, and he returned my look with a lopsided grin. His dark eyes were open and soft as he looked intently into mine. Our eyes stayed locked for a moment before Taylor finally broke the silence.

"Do you mind if I ask you a personal question?"

Here we go.

Now do you see why I couldn't be around these people? It wasn't just because a Normal could get hurt; it was also dangerous for me and my mom. If anything slipped, if any hints were given about us, we would be done for.

"Actually, I—" my response was cut short by the sound of my phone ringing.

Hallelujah.

"Sorry, hold on one sec," I said, scrambling for my phone. I finally found it at the bottom of my purse and answered.

"Hello?" I said.

"Alexis, where are you?" my mother asked from the other end of the line.

"I'm at the park" I replied.

"I want you to head home soon, okay? I'll be working late and I don't want you out running around without me close by," she said sternly.

"Why?" I asked. Seriously, who or what could possibly mess with me?

"It would make me more comfortable. Plus, I said so."

Good gosh, I hated that line. But it didn't bother me as much right then because it gave me a golden opportunity to dodge Taylor's question.

"All right, bye."

Taylor spoke again before I could explain.

"I heard her from here," he said, amused.

I laughed weakly and replied, "Sorry, but I really should get home."

"It's okay; I understand." Taylor stood and offered his hand to help me up. I gladly took his support as I rose from the grass.

"I guess I'll see you around," I said, disappointed that I had to leave but glad I wouldn't have to worry about that personal question.

"Yeah," he agreed, "I'll see you."

Even though we had said goodbye, we continued to stare at each other… and to hold hands.

"Well, bye," I said as I turned to leave.

"Wait," he said, catching my arm before I got too far.

"Yeah?" I asked.

"Let me walk you home," he offered.

I looked at him questioningly. What guy in this day and age walks a girl home? I don't think I'd ever met the chivalrous type before.

"Um, that's okay. I know my way home." I tried to walk away again, but he stopped me.

"You sure? There have been some cougar sightings around this area."

I laughed, thinking that he was joking. Apparently, he wasn't.

"Oh, I think I'll be fine."

"Suit yourself," Taylor said, finally allowing me to make my way home.

I could feel his eyes on me as I walked away from him.

The thing I didn't understand was why he wanted to talk to me. I mean, I didn't know him… at all. Before I ran into him on the sidewalk, he was a complete stranger. For that matter, he still was a stranger!

Then why do I feel so close to him?

It was then that I heard footsteps behind me. Just out of curiosity, I casually glanced over my shoulder to see who it was.

Dang, this boy is persistent.

Taylor noticed my glance and said:

"What? A guy can't walk?" I couldn't help but giggle a little. Just the way he said it made it funny. He grinned as I laughed.

"You know, in some states this would be considered stalking," I called over my shoulder, turning my back to him again. I heard him chuckle softly to himself.

"I'm not walking *with* you. I'm *behind* you. Doesn't count," he said sarcastically.

"True," I said, turning back around. "But who's to say that your motives are different?"

He stopped and asked, "Who said I had motives?"

I couldn't tell if we were still joking or if he had moved onto a more serious question.

I shifted uncomfortably in my spot and asked, "I don't know. Do you?"

Taylor paused for a moment, making the air catch in my chest. He then walked up to me and said, "The only motive I have is to get to know you more."

I looked down at my hands as I asked, "Why would you want to do that?"

He shrugged and said, "I don't know, you're interesting. You seem worth learning more about."

"I'm really not. Trust me," I said, desperately wanting to escape this conversation that had suddenly grown so heavy.

"I think you are," he said kindly.

"Well, I'm not."

"Whatever you say," he surrendered, letting the subject drop.

I turned back around and began walking. But this time, Taylor stayed by my side.

We didn't talk for a few minutes, which should have been awkward but wasn't. I really shouldn't have been walking with him in the first place, but I didn't want to say goodbye either.

"So," he began after a while, "what school do you go to?"

"Chattanooga High, I'm a sophomore there. What about you?" I asked, not able to control myself.

"I'm homeschooled."

"Oh, doesn't that get annoying? Why not go to a regular school?"

He shrugged and said, "Kind of. Mark, my adoptive dad, insists that I can get a better education if he teaches me. But the whole thing sucks pretty bad sometimes."

"Why?" I asked, sincerely interested.

"Picture it like this: It can feel like being taught by a Nazi," he said with a chuckle.

I grinned at Taylor, but mostly because I liked his smile. It wasn't even a full smile—more like a lazy grin—but he rocked it.

There was a long pause between us, with a little bit of awkwardness this time. After a minute, Taylor finally spoke.

"About that personal question..."

My blood ran cold as I thought of what he was about to ask me—or what he wanted from me.

It could be anything...

"What about it?" I asked, trying to sound casual.

"Is it, you know, cool if I ask my question?"

For reasons I still don't understand, I replied, "Sure, I guess."

Taylor looked away, as if trying to word what he wanted to say correctly. Each second it took him to think made my heart crash even harder against my ribcage. If it were any quieter outside, he probably would have been able to hear it.

Finally, he took a deep breath and asked: "Do you have any idea why your dad left?"

Again, his words pulverized my chest—even if he didn't really know what he was asking.

I looked away from his dark eyes and down at my hands. A long moment passed; then he asked another question. "Do you even know who he is?"

I shut my eyes, trying to steady my breaths as I felt my shoulders tremble.

I suddenly felt something warm lightly touch my shoulder. Realizing it was Taylor's comforting hand, my body began to relax.

But it wasn't enough.

My arms and legs were already beginning to tingle; soon, they would be numb.

"Look, I'm sorry I didn't mea—"

"Don't…don't worry 'bout it. No big deal," I lied. "I really need to go. Thanks for kinda walking me home."

I wasn't going to wait for a response, but just as I turned, Taylor said, "No problem. I'll see you tomorrow?"

I turned back to face him. I wondered if he was *asking* me to hang out again or if it was more like a "see you around" kind of statement.

"Um, yeah...see you around," I said.

At least my reply could go either way, too. You know: If he wasn't asking to see me again, I wouldn't sound like an idiot.

He beamed a smile at me—not the lazy grin he had been wearing before. This was the blindingly white smile that had practically hypnotized me that day on the sidewalk.

It was even better than the lazy grin.

I smiled back, but my happiness vanished when I felt my curse become almost too much to handle.

I spun on my heels and began walking as fast as I could without drawing attention to myself. It felt like hours before Taylor was out of my sight. With a quick 360 glance of to make sure I was alone, I slipped into the forest.

As soon as the road was hidden by trees, I knew it was safe to unleash my powers.

☙

Relief flowed over me as my tense shoulders relaxed. The seventh-period bell had finally rung and I was able to go home.

I was the first one out of the classroom door and the first in the hall at my locker. By the time I was ready to go, people were still lingering along the hallway.

There were jocks getting their things together for the big game tonight, girls talking to their friends, and a few couples making out (apparently, they couldn't wait).

I didn't get it. I mean, the bell had rung almost five minutes ago, but people were taking their time. Didn't they want to get out of this place as soon as possible? I shook my head, wondering how people could actually enjoy school. Then again, these were Normals, not freakish superpowered girls like me.

Sighing, I walked through the double doors and outside into the sunny weather. Down two small flights of stairs, and I was on my way home. As I walked along the sidewalk by the parking lot, a car caught my attention; a song by my favorite band could be heard coming from its speakers.

A guy leaned against the side of the car, watching as students passed on the sidewalk. He seemed familiar, so I looked closer.

My heart pounded with excitement when I saw that the guy was Taylor.

Is he waiting for me?

I laughed at myself.

He must have some friends that he's meeting here.

Even though I tried to convince myself otherwise, I still held out a little hope that he had come to see me.

It was then that I realized the danger of what I was thinking.

I couldn't see him again. I'd only been around him twice, and both times, my powers had almost overtaken me. What if I couldn't control myself that day? I wasn't about to take a risk like that with Taylor. I sighed as I continued to stare at him.

Why does he have to be so amazing?

Just then, Taylor glanced in my direction. We made eye contact for a second and he grinned at me.

I looked away, embarrassed that I had been staring. Good thing I stopped when I did, any longer and I might have started drooling. Yeah, there's nothing better than having a hot guy catch you gawking like an idiot.

When I looked back in Taylor's direction, I saw that he was coming my way.

I'll admit it, when I saw Taylor walking across the parking lot, I felt the urge to run toward him and jump into his arms like they do in those cheesy romantic movies.

Hey, just because I'm practically a weapon of mass destruction doesn't mean that I don't have a tender side….

Taylor made it to the sidewalk and stopped at the curb.

"Hey," he said, still grinning.

"Um, what are you doing here?" I asked.

He raised an eyebrow and said, "Nice to see you, too, sunshine."

"I didn't mean it like that," I said, smiling apologetically.

He chuckled and said, "I know. I came here to ask what you're doing after school."

I was surprised by what he said. It took me a minute to answer him.

"Nothing, I was just going home, actually. Why?" I asked, my heart rate speeding up.

"I want to show you something."

I narrowed my eyes and asked, "What is it?"

Taylor beamed his rock-star smile and said, "If I told you, it would ruin the surprise."

I stared at him, wondering what to say to that.

"So, whataya say?" he asked after a moment.

Again, I was faced with that "stay or skedaddle" choice.

Obviously, the idea of going with Taylor was tempting. But, like I said before, both times I had been with him, I'd had to take off before my powers overwhelmed me. On the other hand, I did control myself both times. Well, enough not to hurt him anyway.

I did it twice; I can do it again....

"Sure," I finally said. "Just let me make a quick call."

He smiled even bigger—taking my breath away—and said, "Awesome."

I smiled too as I dug for my phone. I dialed the number I wanted and waited for an answer.

"Hi, Mom? Yeah, I'm going to be late coming home this afternoon."

ℭ

The gentle Tennessee air lightly tossed my hair as Taylor drove his car down the road. With the windows rolled down, I felt much better about being in an enclosed space with him. My claustrophobia and fear of closeness were in the background–for the moment.

"C'mon, at least give me a hint," I begged. We had been driving for over an hour, but Taylor still hadn't given me a clue about what he was up to.

Taylor laughed, amused by my impatience, and said, "Nope, no hints."

"Ugh, you enjoy torturing me, don't you?" I asked.

"You bet," he said, winking at me.

I rolled my eyes at him, trying to disguise the fact that he had just made my heart flutter like crazy.

A few minutes went by before Taylor pulled onto a back road. He parked next to some trees and turned off his car.

"We're here," he said, getting out of the car.

I looked around at the remote area, wondering what in the world he possibly had to show me out in the middle of nowhere.

I reached for the door handle, but Taylor beat me to it. He opened the door and helped me out.

I looked down at my feet for a moment, then glanced at my surroundings.

"So, you wanted to show me...*trees*?" I asked.

He chuckled, pushing some black hair out of his face, and said, "No."

"Well, then, tell me. What is it?"

"I can't really tell you. It's more something I have to *show* you."

"Okay, then, show me," I demanded.

"I will, but there's a bit of a walk ahead of us," he replied, gesturing for me to follow him.

"Okay," I said. As we stepped into the trees, I saw a rocky, barely visible path.

We hiked for a bit before I managed to trip over a rock. Taylor caught me by the arm before I could fall. Once I was steady, he let my arm go and took my hand.

"Sorry, I should have warned you about the path."

"Oh, it's cool," I said as I carefully curled my fingers around his hand, even though I knew I didn't need the support that badly.

After an intense, twenty-minute trek, Taylor stopped and turned to me. Still holding my hand, he said, "Okay, this is what I wanted to show you." With that, he led me through a break in the trees to a small grassy clearing.

"Whoa" was all I could say.

It was beautiful. The grass was bright and healthy, there were wildflowers growing all around, and the sun was beginning to set right before my eyes. I half expected Bambi to come prancing out of the trees with his woodland friends.

Taylor saw the look on my face and gave my hand a little squeeze.

"Come on," he said, leading me farther into the clearing. After just a few feet, the grass ended and I saw that we were on a ledge. It wasn't until I looked down that I finally realized we had hiked up a mountain—*high* up a mountain.

"WHOA," I repeated.

Letting go of my hand, Taylor laughed and walked back toward the middle of the clearing. There was a log on the ground, resting against a tree. Taylor rolled it to the middle of the ledge and said, "I come up here all the time when I need to be alone."

"Oh," I said as I sat on the log. "Then why not leave the log here instead of having to roll it back and forth?"

Taylor sat next to me and said, "I don't want it to roll off the ledge and hit something."

I nodded and looked back up at the sky. It was turning a rich orange color as the sun sank lower and lower into the horizon.

"How did you find this place?" I asked, breaking the silence.

"I like being outside and hiking a lot. I was out on this mountain one day and stumbled across it when the sun was setting. Just like it is now."

"I'm glad you showed me this place; it's gorgeous," I said, still staring at the sky.

Suddenly, I felt Taylor's arm touch mine. I looked back at him and saw that he was staring. His eyes were open and admiring as he said, "I'm glad you came."

I felt my face grow hot and my heart beginning to speed up again. I turned my face back to the sky so he wouldn't see me blushing.

We stayed there—talking and watching—until the sun was completely gone. Night came, and it seemed that the stars were just six feet over our heads. Even then, we stayed a little longer.

Eventually, we decided it would be a good idea to head back home—even though we both felt reluctant to. After Taylor dropped me off at home, and after gushing to Mom about my night, I went and got ready for bed.

As I crawled into my warm covers, I began thinking of my time with Taylor. It wasn't until after replaying the day for the fifth time in my head that I realized something—maybe I *did* have more control than I thought I did. Maybe I *was* learning more about my powers.

Smiling, my eyelids grew heavier and heavier as one single thought echoed through my head:

Maybe I can *do this….*

Chapter 3

It's dark here, I thought. And indeed, it was, very dark. Not only in the sense of having no light but also in the atmosphere. I could feel my frantic eyes searching for something, but what? It seemed like my eyes knew what was going on, but my brain wasn't in on the situation. I extended my arms to feel around for the mysterious object I was searching for. Before I could find whatever it was, I heard an anxious voice in the distance.

"Alexis? Is that you…? Are you there? ALEXIS?!" I recognized this voice.

"Taylor?" There was a short pause; no answer.

"Taylor!" I shouted as loud as I could.

I was panicking. Something was wrong. No, wait, something was out to get me. I had absolutely no idea what was going on, but I knew one thing… I had to find Taylor. I was running in circles to find the source of the voice, but no one appeared.

Then, in the blink of an eye, it was sunny. The ominous atmosphere had lightened as well, but not fully dissipated. I looked around and saw that I was in a familiar place. Here was the middle of my forest, but no trees were broken or smashed. They all stood tall and proud and, somehow, peaceful. The weather was beautiful… a cool autumn day.

After a moment, I came back to my senses and remembered what I was looking for. "TAYLOR!!!" I hollered even louder than before, but my shouts didn't disturb the tranquility of the forest.

"Hi, there," a calm, hypnotic voice said from a few yards behind me. I turned around to meet the gaze of Taylor's mysterious eyes.

He was leaning against a tree with a lopsided grin on his face.

"Taylor!" I exclaimed. I started running to him, but my pace seemed unnaturally slow.

Words could not describe how relieved I was to see that he was safe and, even more, how happy I was that he was here with me. Something was still off about the whole scene, but at the moment, all I cared about was Taylor.

I stopped in front of him and looked up to meet his eyes. He gazed at me with a look of gentleness and caring, and I mirrored his expression. He lifted his big, rough hand and stroked my right cheek lightly with the back of his fingers. Instantly, I felt my face turn bright red and fiery hot. He delicately glided his fingers up and down my face, from my cheekbone to my jaw. I looked deeper into his eyes and saw that they seemed distant and worried.

"Taylor, what's wrong?" I asked in a sweet, compassionate tone (sounding nothing like myself).

His eyes still looked anxious, but he smiled sympathetically and said, "Lex, as long as you're with me, absolutely nothing could be wrong." I beamed with adoration, his words sparking a glow in my heart.

I lifted my hand to stroke his cheek, as he had done to me. At that moment, a breeze blew by that was a bit too chilly for comfort. As my hand moved closer to his face, the scene grew darker and darker. There was hardly enough light to see anything when my hand lightly brushed his cheek. In that very second, I saw panic in his eyes, and an instant later, his image shattered into a million pieces.

"NO!!!" I screamed out in terror. Dropping to my knees, I felt hot tears starting to run down my face. Before I could catch my breath, a sinister chuckle rumbled behind me.

I jumped a good four feet in the air and whirled around to see a dark figure standing between two skinny trees. He was wearing a long black cloak that dragged on the ground behind him.

I had no idea what was going on. Millions of thoughts were rushing through my head, but before I could untangle them, the figure began to speak.

"Well, well, well… It certainly has been a long time, Alexis. Watch your back. We are everywhere and could be *anyone*."

ଓଓଓ

I woke with my heart racing at the speed of light, my whole body moist with sweat, and my breath short and quick. My lungs felt as if they were going to pop, and I swear that my ribs were vibrating as my heart crashed into them. My eyes darted around my room in a panic as my mind tried to recover from the nightmare. A long moment passed before I was even remotely calm.

As my mind settled down, I reached out a shaky hand to turn on my bedside lamp. I glanced at the clock beside me; it was 5:36 in the morning. I didn't have to get up for school until 8:00, so I lay down on my back. My heartbeat was still rapid, but my breathing had slowed. I found myself staring blankly at the ceiling. I think I was still numb from the nightmare. My brain was fresh out of thoughts.

After about fifteen minutes of staring at the ceiling, I finally returned to coherence. "Oh… my gosh," I said aloud. Thoughts were flowing through my mind, logic was coming back into play, and fear was setting in. The images from the nightmare started replaying in my head.

It was completely and utterly horrific. I tried not to think about the part where I… umm… shattered Taylor. But for some reason, that wasn't the part that was most disturbing. It was the dark figure that was freaking me out. It was like I knew who he was, but at the same time, he was unrecognizable. The figure was definitely a grown man, that's for sure, but the forest in my dream was so dark that I couldn't even get a glimpse of his face. Whoever he was, I knew he was no good.

So, I had one of the most amazing times of my life the day before, but, the same night, I get a nightmare about killing Taylor? How that worked, I didn't know.

The harder I thought about it, the harder it was to settle down. I finally gave up on deciphering the dream and tried to fall back asleep. Luckily, it didn't take long. I closed my eyes for one second and, in the next, my mother was by my bedside shaking me awake.

ଓଃ

"Alexis? Lex? Come on… wake up, time for school," my mother said as she continued to poke and shake me.

"Ohhh…. Mom, no," I whined.

I was exhausted from my early-morning brush with terror, and I *really* wasn't in the mood for school.

"Come on, Lex, please, get up." Her tone was pleading and worried. I turned on my right side and slowly opened my eyes to look at my mother. Her face was creased with concern. She looked as if she had had a late night, too.

"Lex, what happened last night? Are you okay?" she asked.

"No—well, yes. I mean, I guess. I just had a nightmare, it shook me up a little."

"What was it about?"

I knew Mom meant well, but the dream really did scare the living crap out of me. So, I wasn't exactly in the mood for a discussion—especially right after I had woken up.

"Mom, I really don't want to talk about it. Just look in my head again so I don't have to explain it to you," I mumbled, resting my forehead against my palm.

"Honey, I wish I could, but I can't." I immediately popped straight up and looked at my mom in confusion.

"What do you mean you can't?" I asked, suddenly alert.

"I mean that your mind is so scrambled that I can't get a clear picture. Late last night, I felt you getting anxious. You're emotions were getting more and more intense up until about 5 in the morning when they just stopped."

Mom paused and took a breath before continuing.

"I assumed you were having a nightmare and was going to check your head this morning. So, I tried right before waking you up. But, when I did I could only tell that you had a nightmare by your emotions, not by your thoughts." She looked at me as if she wanted me to give her every excruciating detail of my nightmare.

Well, we don't always get what we want now, do we?

"Mom, do I have to go to school?"

She only gave me a little snort in response.

"I'm serious. I really can't go today. Please don't make me!" I was begging. I know it sounds pathetic, but it was my only chance.

"Alexis, you have to go."

"No, Mom! Please don't make me! *Please*?" I was on the verge of tears, and when I get angry or upset, I can't control myself. Right then, I was imagining myself at school, a nervous wreck.

Trust me… it is not a pretty thing to see. It's bad enough when I get angry, but when I'm having an emotional breakdown…

"What kind of a mother would I be if I let you cut school just because you had a bad dream?"

"A smart one," I mumbled in a tone that I shouldn't have used with my mother.

"Lose the attitude, young lady. Get up, get ready, and go to school," she fired back.

I stared at her with cold eyes, trying to fight back the tears that were ready to gush out. After a moment, she got up and walked out of my room without saying another word. As she shut the door, I tried to take deep breaths—in and out—to calm myself. When I felt a little more in control, I threw the covers off my bed and slowly walked to my bathroom, still fighting back tears, and started to get ready.

It usually takes me only about fifteen minutes, maybe even less, to go through my morning routine. I was halfway out the bathroom door, thinking about what I would wear, when I stopped. I went back to my mirror and carefully inspected my hair and face.

"Hmmm… I guess it wouldn't hurt to put on a little more makeup," I said aloud.

I smoothed on some extra foundation, added a little eyeliner, and beefed up the mascara. I put some anti-frizz gel in my hair and decided to straighten it. When I took a final look at myself, I was pleasantly surprised with how well my efforts had turned out.

I walked out of my bathroom and into my room to change. I usually pull a pair of old jeans and a t-shirt out of my dresser, but on that day, I wanted an outfit that would go with my flawless makeup and perfectly styled hair.

I walked over to my closet, where I keep my nicer clothes, the ones I rarely wear because they seem too fancy or dressy. But today was an exception.

I don't even know why I have all these clothes; I never wear them. My mom loves to buy me things, and I appreciate it, but sometimes, she gets a little carried away.

I considered and rejected a number of outfits in my search for the perfect look. All the clothes were beautiful and flattering, but I finally settled on my favorite.

I changed into my baby-doll top and pulled on some black leggings. Then I slipped on my gray ballet flats. I looked at myself, yet again, in my full-length mirror, twirling and turning while I inspected the results.

I found a thick gold belt hanging in the closet and attached it around my waist. I also managed to dig up a small necklace in the same shade of gold.

I went back to my mirror for the finishing touches.

"ALEXIS!" I jumped when I heard my mother scream my name from the other room.

"WHAAT!?" I screamed back.

"YOU'RE GOING TO BE LATE! GET YOUR BUTT DOWN HERE!" She sounded as pissed off as I had been earlier. I followed her orders and hurried through my final touches.

I snagged a small purse, grabbed my cell phone, and rushed out of my room. I walked into the living room, where my mother was pacing impatiently back and forth. She raised her voice to yell for me again.

"ALEX—" but before she could finish my name, she noticed that I was standing in front of her.

Her eyes grew wide and her mouth dropped open.

"What?" I asked in a worried tone. "Is there something on my face? Is there something wrong with my clothes?" She blinked a few times before speaking.

"No… it's just that… you look beautiful. I mean, you always do, but today… wow."

"Really? Are you sure it's not too much?" I gestured to the clothing with my hand as I asked.

"Oh no, not at all, Lex! Taylor is going to be blown away." She smiled excitedly when she spoke.

"Mom, what makes you think I'm doing this for him?" She rolled her eyes, and I felt my face grow hot. "Because I'm not!" I said, trying to recover.

"Uh-huh… sure," my mother said smugly. "Do you want a ride to school?"

"No, thanks, I'm just going to run." Mom gave me a confused look.

"Are you serious? It took you so long to get ready… are you sure?" she asked. Even with her mind-reading powers, there were some things my mother just couldn't figure out about me.

"Yeah, I'm sure. I think a good run and fresh air will do me some good before school starts." Obviously, I had other reasons for wanting to go to school on my own, and my mother knew it, but she didn't bother to argue with me.

"All right, if that's what you want," she began, "but don't get your hair and makeup messed up while you're running; then all that time primping will be a big waste," she said in a teasing tone.

"Ha. Okay, Mom. I'll be home right after school." I gave her a quick hug and said goodbye, then grabbed my backpack and threw it over my right shoulder. Once I was out the door and onto the porch, I paused, checking out the forest that surrounds our house.

I don't know why, but I always like to scan the area every day before school. I'm not quite sure what I'm looking for, but I guess I'll know it when I see it.

Maybe I'm afraid that our house will be discovered, but we're pretty well hidden, and no one, not even the school administration, knows where our house *really* is.

A short distance from the house is a mailbox in front of a random dirt trail. The dirt trail goes on forever. If you tried to follow it, you wouldn't find anything but trees. The address on that mailbox is where our house supposedly is. All our bills and letters and such are sent there—pretty clever, huh?

After a minute or two of gazing into the trees, I ran full speed down the usual path to school, thinking about what I might say to Taylor if I saw him.

I don't even know if he likes me like that. He barely knows me! What if he's not there today? Or even worse… what if he is there and he thinks I'm some kind of stalker?

I stopped dead in my tracks. I had not even considered the fact that he might not want to see me.

It took me a minute to come back to my *real* senses and realize exactly what I was doing.

"UGH! What is wrong with me?!" I growled aloud.

I shouldn't even be thinking about him, let alone trying to talk to him! He's a Normal!

My heart was beginning to race and my hands were clenched into fists. I knew I was running late, but I needed to calm myself down. In a desperate attempt to rid myself of anger, I turned around and punched a tree. My powerful fist blew a giant crater in the dark trunk. Splinters went flying, and the tree instantly fell to the ground.

I turned back around and sprinted off to school. As I was running, I looked down to see my bleeding knuckles, which were already starting to swell. I grimaced at my own stupidity and kept running, feeling no pain.

Soon enough, I was only a few yards away from the exact spot where I had collided with Taylor the other day. I started to slow down, debating with myself about whether I should keep running or stop.

I knew what I wanted to do, but I didn't know if it was right. I might put him in danger if I saw him again, but I still couldn't help wanting to stop and wait. Maybe he came by here every day.

Almost instinctively, my legs came to a dead halt in the exact spot where I had met Taylor.

☙

Two minutes passed and I didn't see him, but I wasn't worried... yet.

ᘛ

Five minutes passed and I still didn't see him. I was getting anxious.

ᘛ

Ten minutes passed and I *still* didn't see him. I was starting to freak out.

ᘛ

Fifteen minutes passed… Still no Taylor! Now I was pissed.

ᘛ

Twenty minutes passed and my heart had had enough.

Chapter 4

He didn't show. He didn't show.... The same thought kept repeating in my head. As nervous and unsure as I had been that morning, I really thought that Taylor would be in the same spot where we had met. Something in my heart told me that he *should* have be there.

I stood still as a statue, frozen in place. I was trying hard to fight back tears. My muscles felt tense with stress and my stomach was queasy with anxiety. I couldn't flex anything; I was literally locked in place.

Pull it together, Lex... just calm down. But that was much easier said than done. I managed to work my hand into my purse and get my cell phone. I checked the time, not that I cared whether I made it to school or not. It was 8:57 and I was about to be late. The only thing keeping me from not going to school at all was my mom. To tell you the truth, she scares the bejesus out of me when she's pissed. She would kill me if I was late again.

Of course, I didn't have enough time to race back to the forest and punch a tree to calm myself down. My only option was to run as fast as I possibly could and hope that I got to school on time and could relieve some anger on the way. I doubted whether it would work, but it was worth a shot.

I shook my head to clear my mind, bent down into a crouch position so that I could take off at a reasonable speed, and glanced around to see whether anyone was watching me. When I was sure that I was alone, I took off.

As I ran, my arms and legs felt numb, and I still wasn't completely focused. My head felt fuzzy, as if I was jacked up on way too much cold medicine.

Running at an implausible speed, I tried to comfort myself. *It's not the end of the world… maybe he was there earlier and I missed him… maybe he'll be there later….* With that thought, I stopped.

Maybe he will be there after school! I mean, that's when we met the other day, and I was running really late. Who knows? Maybe he waited there this morning. Yeah! That's it! I just missed him; that's all. He'd be there later.

Maybe it was true; maybe it was wishful thinking. But whatever gets you through the day, right?

Soon enough, I was at the back entrance of my school. I approached the door and drew in a shallow breath. I walked down the long, lonely hallway that led to my locker so that I could put my books away and grab what I needed for first period. As I shut the locker door, I took a careful look up and down the hallway to see if it was safe to sprint to class. Then, I heard an unfamiliar voice.

"Excuse me, young lady!" a man called from down the hall in a stern and short-tempered tone. I immediately turned to look at him as he marched toward me like the commander-in-chief of some army. His fists were balled up, his jaw was clenched, and his eyebrows etched hard lines on his forehead.

I felt as if I knew this man from somewhere. Given that my school was so big, it was possible that I'd seen him around without realizing it. But something told me that I knew him from somewhere else, somewhere not associated with school. I felt as if I *should* be able to place him, but I couldn't. I cocked my head in confusion and examined him further.

He was a short man, but he wasn't stubby. He wore blue jeans and a short-sleeved polo shirt that showed off his muscular arms. He also had a lean, fit body. He reminded me of a compact tank. I guessed that he was no more than forty, tops.

I was still trying to figure out how I knew him when I realized he was standing in front of me with his arms crossed and his foot tapping.

"Ahem, miss? I asked you where you were going. Answer the

question." I shook my head and readjusted my focus, looking directly at him.

"Oh… umm… I was going to… umm—" He cut me off before I could finish explaining.

"I don't have time for funny business, and I know *you* don't have time for lollygagging in the halls while class is in session." He spoke in a stern and authoritative manner, staring down at me with furious eyes.

"I– I– I'm sorry. I… was just going to class." I stammered like an idiot.

Real smooth, Alexis.

This guy was really making me nervous. I can't think of a time when I've been afraid of a Normal, but here was an exception. The only person who usually makes me even remotely anxious is my mother. But this guy seemed to have a hostile and violent aura. He looked like he'd be willing to expel me, or worse, just for being late.

"It didn't seem like you were hurrying to class to me. What is your name?" he asked.

"Alexis," I said in a small voice.

"Alexis?" He paused for a moment. "Alexis," he continued aloud in a hushed tone. He took his gaze off me and stared into space, rubbing his chin with his hand.

Then, his eyes snapped open in shock. He looked back at me, his expression no longer angry or hostile. I can only describe it as fervent.

"Alexis Randall?" he asked. He tried to keep his voice under control, but his words were quick and excited.

"Yes sir," I replied, bringing my books closer to my chest.

His expression then melted from excitement to something mischievous and slightly sinister. He raised one eyebrow, and his eyes seemed to relax. He put on a crooked grin and loosened his balled-up fists at his sides. He crossed his arms and leaned his shoulder against the locker next to mine.

"Alexis Randall… Alexis Randall…." He laughed quietly as he repeated my name.

"I'm sorry, but have we met before?" I was confused.

Why does it seem like… he knows me?

Then, he chuckled, and I froze. My heart stopped beating for a few seconds, my hands started to moisten, and my breathing came in short bursts. He seemed to find amusement in my sudden anxiety.

"Well, I guess it has been a long time…," he said, sidling closer to me. Instinctively, I pulled back. "How disappointing. I was hoping you would remember me." He made a fake sad face that sent chills down my spine. Then he stared at me with big blue eyes as he inched his way toward me.

"You're nervous," he said. He was still staring intensely into my eyes. I was hyperventilating now and numb all over. I turned away and started running. My class was just at the end of the hall, but I couldn't get there fast enough.

I didn't even bother to turn around to see if the creep was following me. I didn't hear any footsteps behind me, so I figured he was still at the locker.

When I reached the door of my class, I wrapped my hand around the knob but took one final look back before entering.

The scary guy hadn't moved an inch, and his eyes were still locked on me. He held my gaze for a few seconds before breathing out a sinister laugh.

I flung open the door and escaped into the room. When I slammed the door shut, the frame rattled and the glass shook.

I turned around to see the entire class staring at me. A few were laughing quietly to themselves or whispering to their friends. Others shot me weird looks. Of course, my teacher just seemed irritated.

"So nice of you to join us, Ms. Randall. Please take your seat." I took my usual spot in the back corner of the room. I crammed my things into the rack under my desk and tried to settle myself so that I could focus on the lesson.

I was still flustered by that creep in the hall, but I tried to bury my fear and forget about the whole encounter.

☙

School days for me are usually slow, but this was ridiculous! First period felt like it was three hours long, second period was just as bad, and it was only the beginning of third period. It seemed like I had been at school for eight hours, but it was only 11:00.

I entered my third-period class and sat down right away in the back corner. I was one of the first ones in class, so only a few students were in the room, standing and talking.

I couldn't help but look over my shoulder every few seconds. I was still majorly creeped out by my encounter with that guy.

Slowly, the other students trickled in. With about thirty seconds left to get to class, a swarm of students rushed through the door and took their seats.

Our teacher wasn't yet in the room, so the students took the opportunity to chat with their friends. The class became very loud, and I began to get irritated.

I tried to focus on my breathing, a trick my mom taught me to keep my cool, but it didn't seem to work very well.

Finally, our history teacher, Ms. Garner, walked into the class and silenced us. Following her was a boy who looked about my age. I wondered who he was.

"Class, settle down, please." The talking in the room slowly subsided.

"I apologize for being tardy, but we have a new student starting today. Class, this is Andrew Marion." She gestured with her hand toward Andrew.

Andrew was definitely in my grade because this was strictly a sophomore class. He had sandy blonde hair and light blue eyes. He was cute, I guess, but he seemed like a player. The look of arrogance on his face and the way he strutted into the room like he was ready for the paparazzi to come out and snap his picture was enough to make me immediately not like him.

Andrew scanned the room and his fellow students as if he was completely uninterested in the entire situation.

Ms. Garner said, "All right, Andrew, there are a few seats open in the class; you may choose from any of those available."

"Cool. Thanks," he said smoothly.

He began to walk down the aisle next to mine. There were plenty of seats in the row, but he passed by each one of them, as if he'd already made up his mind about where he wanted to sit. As he passed each empty desk, sighs and huffs came from the surrounding girls, who were hopeful that he would sit next to them.

He finally arrived at a desk and took his seat.

The problem was that it was the one right next to me! *Perfect,* I thought, *as if this day could get any more difficult.*

My teacher had walked back to her desk to check her e-mail.

"Oh darn. Class? I'm sorry, but I completely forgot that I was supposed to go speak to the guidance counselor for a few minutes. While I'm gone, you may talk quietly among yourselves."

Ms. Garner was obviously out to get me.

She walked quickly into the empty hallway. After a few seconds, the room filled with chatter and gossip. I immediately took out my book and started reading the chapter we had been discussing the day before.

I tried hard to concentrate on the book in front of me, but it was difficult given that I was having my second creep encounter of the day.

Andrew's eyes burned into my skin like lasers. I could almost feel him staring at me. It was both weird and annoying. If he had a problem with me, why couldn't he just come right out and say it?

"Hey, I'm Andy." Crap. I didn't mean I wanted him to *talk* to me!

"Maybe you wanna tell me your name… and give me your number?" he asked.

I kept my eyes on the text and didn't bother to respond.

Andrew kept looking at me, expecting me to answer him. He finally spoke up again.

"…or maybe I'll give you mine… if you're down with that."

"No, thanks," I said.

"Oh, I get it. Playin' hard to get? That's cool. I can roll with that," he responded. He leaned back in his chair and put both hands behind his head.

I breathed heavily in and out.

"No, I am *not* playing hard to get, but I'm not giving you my number either," I said, a little louder and a little sterner.

"That's fine, then; I'll just give you mine," he answered. The corners of his mouth rose into a smug grin.

"No, you will not." Now I was getting really irritated.

"But how will you be able to call me if you don't have my number?" he asked.

You've got to be joking.

I looked up for the first time since Andy had started talking to me.

"Don't you have anything better to do than bug the crap out of me?" I fired back harshly.

"Oh, I'm sorry." He leaned closer to me while he spoke. "I didn't realize I was bothering you." By now, he was so close to me that our arms were almost touching.

"I would really appreciate it if you would get out of my face," I said through my teeth.

He opened his mouth to speak, but before he could say another word, I turned my head to face him. I glared at him and he began to back away slightly. At that moment, Mrs. Garner returned to the classroom. She told us to open our textbooks, and we finally began the lesson.

Lucky for Andy.

☙

After third-period history class, I had lunch in the back corner of the cafeteria. I was finally starting to calm down when Andy came up to my table.

"Hey, I know we got off on the wrong foot, but do yah mind if I sit here?"

I really couldn't take much more of this.

"Nope." I got up and started walking away. "It's all yours," I said as I made my way toward the door.

He called out to me as I was walking away, "Come on! Don't be like that!" but I was already gone before he could finish.

After lunch, I had fifth-period biology with good old bizarre Mr. McCormick. It was a tough class, but I got by pretty well. Even so, the teacher was such a freak that I dreaded walking into his room. I never asked questions because then he would drop everything and stand extremely close to me. Needless to say, it's uncomfortable. At least Andy wasn't in biology.

☙

My mood was bad enough already, but it turned from bad to worse when I found out that he *was* in my sixth-period Spanish class.

UGH! This kid was like an annoying fly droning around my head. He was impossible to swat, and that buzzing sound in my ears was driving me slowly insane.

I sat in my usual seat and took out my homework. Andy was at the teacher's desk, waiting to receive his seat assignment. I was kind of in a daze, staring off into space, until I realized something terrible. Once again, the seat next to me was free.

I gripped the desk with my right hand, making finger indentions in the wood, and yanked my notebook out of my backpack with my left. Of course, when I looked up, the teacher was pointing to the desk next to mine. Andy looked over and smiled at me.

I looked down at my notebook and started reviewing for that day's test.

I knew the material already. I just didn't want Andy to talk to me.

Maybe there was a chance he wouldn't bug me… maybe he finally got the hint.

Now *that* was just wishful thinking.

"Hey there, long time no see," he said, leaning in as he sat down. Just then my teacher, Señora Garcia, spoke up.

"*Buenos tardes, sientete por favor.*" After she repeated herself four times, the students followed her instructions slowly and hesitantly. (Half the class never knew what she was saying anyway.)

"What the heck is she talkin' about?" Andy whispered to me.

"Shh," I whispered back harshly.

Our teacher explained what would be on the test. At least, I think that's what she was talking about. I didn't hear a word she said because Andy was trying to flirt with me the entire time she was giving instructions.

When Señora Garcia finished, she passed out the tests, told us to take our time, and left us alone to work. Of course, Andy didn't have to take the test since it was his first day. But instead of getting a head start on the next chapter, as Señora Garcia had suggested, he decided to spend his time doing something else.

While I was taking the test, I could see out of the corner of my eye that he was writing something down. He wasn't doing an assignment—that I was sure of—but he wasn't just doodling either. It was a long note. Oh great, I knew who *that* was for.

I finished my test quickly, but before I got up to turn it in, I sneaked a quick glance at Andy. He was looking at me impatiently, as if he had been waiting for me to finish. I had heard something tapping while I was taking the test, and when I looked at him, I figured out what it was.

It was the piece of paper he had been writing on, now folded neatly and clutched in his hand. He had been tapping the edge of the paper almost the entire time. I knew that the second I returned to my seat after turning in my test, he would try to shove that note right in my face.

I looked back down at my test and erased the entire front page. I began to rewrite the foreign words, neater this time. I examined each every question and answer carefully, at least five times each. Then I repeated the process several times. After about twenty-five minutes, I looked up to see that all the other students had finished.

"Alexis? *Que pasa*?" asked Señora Garcia. I knew exactly what she meant, but I really wasn't in the mood for foreign conversation, so I answered in English.

"What do you mean?" I asked, which seemed to annoy her.

"Alexis, you are finished. I have seen you rewrite your answers almost three times now. Hand in your test, *por favor*." I stared at her hand and reluctantly gave her my completed test.

"*Gracias*. Now class, I really do not have much planned for today, so I'm going to give you a little break. You may choose to start looking at the next chapter on your own, or you may buddy up. You may talk freely, but please try to learn *something*."

Had I missed a memo? "Attention, all school personnel. Today is Torture Alexis Day. Please try to make this day as difficult for her as possible."

"We teachers have to meet with the guidance counselor today to discuss scheduling options for next year. I will be out of the classroom for a few minutes, but I trust you will behave yourselves. Of course, if you get too loud, Senor McGuire is right next door and would be happy to come in and babysit. Are there any questions?" There was a long pause. "All right then," she said, "be good while I'm gone."

Of course, once she was out of the room, the class immediately burst into conversation. Desks were pulled together, some people stood up and moved around the room, and others plopped down in circles on the floor.

I opened my book to begin reading the chapter when Andy lightly touched my arm. I jerked away instinctively and glared at him.

"What the—what is your problem?" I asked in a hard voice. I was getting pissed off beyond belief. I knew if I didn't get a hold of myself soon, there would be a big mess to clean up later.

"Sorry!" he said defensively, then, "Here." He held the folded piece of paper in his outstretched hand.

I took the paper and looked at it in disbelief. My eyes grew wide and my mind went blank. After a second or two, the hand holding the note started shaking uncontrollably. It clenched into a fist so tight that had the paper been a brick, I would have crumbled it to dust. I threw the note into my opened textbook and slammed it shut, producing a loud BOOM that echoed throughout the room.

My thoughts were growing violent and dangerous.

Oh. My. Gosh. I am going to kill him. I mean it. He is dead. He will die now! He will be so sorry that he messed with me. I was completely consumed by anger.

All logic and awareness evaporated. I had no control of my thoughts. All I could think was I was going to murder Andy.

Soon, I would not be able to control my body. I had a death grip on both sides of my desk, my whole body was rigid, and my breathing had turned into snarling.

"Hey, just chill…" he began. He reached out and put his hand on my arm as he spoke. I was about to explode, ready to destroy not only him but everyone and everything else in the room.

"You have exactly five seconds to get your hand off of my arm!" I half shouted, half growled at him. He immediately jerked his hand away and held up both his palms.

"What is your problem?" he asked, bewildered by my behavior. There was a long pause before I spoke.

"Do you *really* wanna know what my problem is? *Really?*" I asked in a taunting tone. I turned to face him and saw that his eyes had grown wide with terror.

"DO YOU REALLY HAVE TO ASK?!" I was shouting now because I was totally and completely enraged. I was ready to kill, to destroy, but somehow, I managed to hold myself together just a little bit longer. Unfortunately, in a situation like this, longer isn't always long enough.

It had gotten eerily quiet just then—obviously the other students noticed the disturbance and were waiting for something to happen. I couldn't see them, though. They were merely blurred globs of color in my peripherals. I could see them shift and move, but other than that, I wasn't paying much attention to them—at least I wouldn't until I was through with Andy.

He held the edge of his desk with one hand and gripped the back of his seat with the other. He knew that I was infuriated, and he may have even sensed that he was in danger, but he didn't understand the full reality of his situation.

"Hey, seriously, you need to take it easy!" Andy tried to sound stern, but his voice sounded shaky and defenseless.

His fear was sickly satisfying to me. The panic in his eyes, the tremor as he spoke, and the terror on his face were almost amusing. I couldn't help but smile a little bit at Andy's terror. My eyes were locked on his image like a missile locked on its target, and I was definitely ready to fire away.

My smile disintegrated and I felt myself begin to rise from my seat. As I slowly straightened up, Andy leaned away from me.

"I– I– I'm warning you! Get away from me!" Andy shouted at me.

Of course, there's nothing he can do. He's nothing more than a defenseless little Normal and I am the ultimate in destruction. He doesn't stand a chance against me… not in this lifetime.

My thoughts were getting out of hand and my mind could no longer hold back my body. My powers now controlled me.

My body suddenly snapped into a cat-like crouching position with my hands extended in front of me. My eyes narrowed, my hands tensed, and my lips slowly curled into a terrifying smile. The scariest part about looking back on that day is that I think I was actually enjoying the fact that Andy's life was going to end at any second.

The next thing I knew, my body was leaping through the air, with my mind set on attacking the boy with the fearful blue eyes and his arms in front of his face.

Chapter 5

I woke up cold and confused. I was sprawled on a large bed in a vaguely familiar room. I had a terrible headache, and my body was limp and exhausted. My eyes were blurry, my mouth was dry, and my head was empty. I had no idea what had happened or what was happening in the present moment. I don't think I even remembered my name or where I lived.

I sat up slowly and sluggishly, looking at the clock on a small TV. It was about 5:00 in the evening. I yawned heavily and lay back down in the comfortable bed. I closed my eyes and slowly drifted into a serene sleep.

As I dozed, thought and logic returned to my brain. I remembered where I was, who I was, and my past. I felt as if I was taking a peaceful stroll down memory lane, until my dreamy recollections turned into tragic, deadly nightmares.

I dreamed that Taylor never wanted to see me again. I also dreamed that I had been angry at school all day. And then… that I had killed a boy I barely knew. The memories became increasingly vivid and clear… the boy, the fear, the anger… it was all so fresh and real. I was positive that I was having a nightmare, but that didn't stop me from snapping awake and screaming. Within seconds of my shriek, my mother was in my room, on her knees, next to my bed.

"Alexis, honey, what's wrong?" she asked in a soothing tone. She held my hand tightly in one of hers, while with the other, she gently stroked my knotted hair. I gulped and panted before I could respond.

"I– I– I had a nightmare. It was awful," I said, out of breath.

"What was your nightmare about?" she asked. I swallowed hard and took a moment to calm myself before speaking.

"I got too angry at school… and I hurt someone." I was ready to cry now, but I held back the tears so I could listen to my mother. I wish I hadn't stopped myself so I wouldn't have had to hear what she said next.

"Alexis," she crooned to me, "that wasn't a nightmare." At that moment, my heart was stricken with pure terror. A sensation of cold shot through my bloodstream, my body froze, and I began to sob uncontrollably. My mother wiped the stream of tears away with her gentle fingers.

"What?" I asked, shocked. "Someone is dead because of me?!" I looked at her incredulously.

"No, no," she quickly said. "He's not dead, thank God, but he is seriously injured." Mom paused for a minute to let me take the news in before continuing. "He's in a deep coma due to serious brain damage. It doesn't seem like he's going to wake up from it anytime soon, but there's a slight chance he will."

I couldn't believe it. I had actually put an innocent person into a coma. Even if he was annoying, I could have… I should have gone home! I knew I was getting angry, but I stayed anyway. I just sat in class like an idiot and let the anger take over. I allowed the curse to control me. Why hadn't I walked out of the classroom? Why did I sit there while Andy pestered me?

I hammered my mother with questions: How did it happen, when did it happen, and how had I ended up at home in bed?

"But Mom," I began, "why don't I remember it? Why can I only see it as a nightmare?" My mother was prepared to answer, but I continued: "Did this happen at school? Why can't I remember even being at school? How long have I been asleep?" I was talking so fast that I was surprised my mom understood even half of what I said. She drew in a deep breath before explaining.

"You were in school, but I could sense your anger and hostility growing as the day went on. I was a little worried, but I figured you could handle it. Then, during the afternoon, I sensed your powers growing to a dangerous level, so I rushed to school right away. I found your Spanish class and walked in at the exact moment that you pounced on that poor boy. Your power levels were off the charts, and there was no way I could calm you down, so I had to shut down your mind. But when I finally did… it was too late." She looked at the floor when she finished.

"Mom, I'm so sorry. This is all my fault. I should have run out of there the minute I felt myself getting too angry."

My mother looked up at me and replied, "Actually, honey, I'm the one who's at fault."

"What, Mom? That's ridiculous…" I said, but she cut me off.

"You tried to warn me this morning, and I didn't listen. I shouldn't have sent you to school in the first place. I'm sorry, Alexis." I stared down at the comforter on my bed.

"Mom, what about the other kids in the room?"

"I wiped their memories. They don't remember anything from that period, and they've never even heard of that boy. As far as his parents know, he was skateboarding to school when he was hit by a car."

"What happens now? Am I just supposed to go back to school and pretend that nothing happened?"

"According to the administration—and me—you no longer attend that school."

If I had heard this at any other time, I would have been bouncing up and down with joy, but now was definitely not a time for celebration.

After a long pause, I finally asked the question my mother had probably been trying to answer herself.

"What are we going to do?" I asked. There was a very long, very quiet pause before she spoke.

"Obviously, we have to move, find a new town, find a new house, and find a new school…" Before she could finish, I shot out from under the covers and glared at her.

"You cannot be serious!" I said in a hard voice.

"What do you mean? We can't stay here."

"That's not it, Mom. How can you even consider putting me back in a school? Have you lost your mind? After what happened today, do you honestly think it's a good idea for me to go to school?!" I was angry again, but of course, my mother wasn't in any danger.

"Honey, I think it's the best thing for you to..." I could not believe what I was hearing; I couldn't even let her finish her sentence.

I stormed out of the room and into the hallway.

"Where in the world are you going?" my mother called out to me from my room.

"I'm getting some air. I have my cell phone," I called back.

I went into the kitchen and found my purse. I yanked it open, grabbed my phone, and walked back to the main hall. I was at the front door with my hand already on the handle. Before opening the door, I looked back down the hallway, where my mother was standing.

She stood stiffly in the middle of the door frame, her arms across her chest. Her head hung low, but her sad eyes were still on me. The look she wore on her face was one I will never forget. She seemed lost, cold, and apologetic all at the same time. My mother had never looked this way to me, and it made me uneasy. I had to turn away because her expression upset me so much.

"I'll be back in a few hours." Those were the last words I said before I ran out the door.

☙

The trees were nothing more than green and brown blurs as I raced through the muggy forest. Several rocks, small and large, were crushed under my feet as I sprinted faster and faster. A slow, depressing rain fell gently from the dark evening sky.

My face was wet with a mixture of rain, tears, and sweat. I had been running for six hours nonstop and must have lapped the forest at least four hundred times. Finally, I headed toward my clearing to lie down.

I was only about halfway there when I was overcome by exhaustion. But I pushed myself to keep going. About thirty seconds later, I was in the clearing. The minute I set foot there, the trees whirled, the earth seemed to slip from underneath my feet, and I fell to the ground.

I think I blacked out for a minute or two, but I came back around… sort of. While I was out, I relived moments of the nightmare I'd had with Taylor in the clearing.

I didn't get to see the happy beginning of my dream, only the terrifying ending. I saw the anxiety in Taylor's eyes when I leaned closer to him. I could actually feel his fear. I watched again as his face shattered. The last thing I saw was the shadow of the mysterious man between the two tall oak trees.

The incident at school began to come back to me as well. I felt the rage, the power, and the desire to kill. Although I was knocked out before I saw what I did to Andy, my mind still managed to give me a clear image.

I suddenly snapped back to consciousness, feeling as if I had taken a horror ride through my own personal hell. I immediately popped straight up, gasping for air. The forest around me was spinning. My eyes were wide and wild with fear, and my mind raced.

To restrain myself, I wrapped my arms around my legs and hugged them tightly. I was shaking uncontrollably, my lungs were on fire, and my eyes felt swollen from crying. My chin rested on my knees as I stared blankly at the trees in front of me.

I was surrounded by hundreds of trees, but now I focused on two specific ones. These particular two trees seemed very familiar—the way they stood, the directions their branches stretched, and the different tones of brown on their trunks. They looked like oaks to me, but I could have been wrong.

Ten minutes must have passed as I stared at the two trees. What was so special about them?

"Wait a minute…" I whispered to myself. I lifted my head from my knees and sat straight up, my arms still wrapped around my legs.

After a few more seconds of intense study, I realized where I had seen the trees before.

I leaped straight up in the air and took off running in the opposite direction. I didn't even give myself time to think about where I was running to. The clearing had once been my sanctuary; now, I wanted to get as far away from it as I could.

After only a few seconds, my lungs were ready to explode. My chest felt as if it was going to tear open, my heart was skipping beats, and the muscles in my legs were burning. Every breath I took was like sucking in fire. The burn strained my throat and seemed to deteriorate the lining of my lungs.

I whimpered and whined as I ran, usually a prelude to crying. But now, no tears fell from my scorching face. My body was completely dry of fluids.

I felt myself grow numb. My eyes were beginning to blur and my vision went black around the edges. My body was shutting down. Unlike the sudden blackout I'd had a few minutes ago in the clearing, this one seemed slow and almost peaceful.

My legs grew weak and I felt myself gradually stop running. I must have been taking in air, but I could no longer feel my fiery breaths or my shriveled lungs. There was no pain—emotional or physical—only numbness. A few minutes later, I found myself on the ground, lying peacefully in the wet, soft grass. The scene around me was blurred but not completely indistinguishable. After a moment, my eyes began to close and I allowed my mind and body to rest.

☙

A worried voice in the distance grew closer and closer.

"Alexis… ALEXIS?! Alexis, honey, are you awake?" It was my mother, I think. She sounded panicked and out of breath as she tried to wake me.

I knew I was awake, and I could hear her, but I couldn't find the energy to open my eyes and tell her I was all right. Or maybe I didn't tell her that because I *wasn't* all right. I was a wreck. All my worst nightmares had come true in a single day. I felt as if I had lost control of my life. I had no idea what to expect next—physically or emotionally. I was caught in a chain of one horrifying experience after another.

My body was weak and vulnerable, something I had never felt before. It frightened me. My legs were sore and tender, my arms were limp, and my face blazed with heat. My stubborn eyelids refused to open when I wanted them to, and my body rejected the idea of moving.

At first, I was afraid that I had been paralyzed or had lapsed into a coma. Just then, a wave of ice-cold water startled me. My body flinched and shivered from the touch of the arctic water. My eyelids immediately popped open, and I leaped into the air. I jumped so high that my head hit the ceiling (making a nice indention), then crashed back down into something hard, cold, and half filled with water.

"Owww," I moaned in pain, rubbing the top of my head. I looked around wearily to find that I was in the bathtub. I turned to look at my mother, standing over me with an empty bucket in her hand.

"Alexis!" she breathed in relief. She got on her knees and hugged me gently.

"Wha…. why am I in the bathtub?" I asked hazily.

"You were overheated and passed out, so I had to dump cold water on you until your temperature went down. I waited for you to wake up, but you took too long, so I panicked and dumped one more bucket on you. Thank God it worked!" She grabbed me again and squeezed me a little harder this time. "I was so worried! What were you doing out there?" I winced at the thought of what had happened out in the forest.

"Umm… I don't really remember," I lied. I was well aware of what had happened.

"Try to remember, honey," my mother encouraged. When I hesitated, she pushed: "Tell me what happened—please?"

"Mom, can I sleep first? I think it will come back to me easier if I let my body rest a while." My mother actually bought it.

"Of course, you can, Alexis," she said gently. The smile on her face was relieved and grateful, but her eyes were anxious and foggy. I think she was trying to see what has going on in my head, but she was having no luck.

"Let me help you," she said and offered both of her arms for stability as I arose from the extremely cold water.

She helped me out of the tub and put two towels around me. One of them was wrapped around my chest and the other hung limply over my shoulders. She helped me into dry pajamas and led me to my room.

I felt heavy as I walked down the hallway. My heart was sunken like a ship at the bottom of an unforgiving ocean. My brain was merely a worn muscle inside my thoughtless head. I felt defenseless and childish—I couldn't even make a journey of six feet down a hall without my mother to hold me up. In a single day, I had gone from a rage-filled monster to a bottomless pit of unsolved problems and surging emotions.

Mom led me into my room and up to the bed. I tried to lift myself into its sweet comfort, but my arms were useless. Mom helped me into bed and gently tucked me in. She kissed my forehead swiftly before making her way for the door.

"Sweet dreams, Alexis," she said meaningfully as she closed the door behind her. Before I could respond, my head involuntarily turned to the side and my eyelids slowly and heavily closed.

Maybe if I'm lucky, my mind will be too tired to have any nightmares tonight. Before surrendering my will power to stay awake, I said a quick prayer. Then I curled up and hoped for peaceful dreams.

Chapter 6

I woke from another restless night. My room was lit, as if I had slept with the lights on all night. My vision was blurred, but despite the light, I couldn't see. I blinked and rubbed my tired eyes, trying to regain clear sight.

After a moment, I was able to see that I was in a strange room. It was a bedroom, with my furniture in it, but it was not my room. The walls here were a pasty pink color instead of pale yellow. The comforter on my bed was now baby blue, unlike my richly colored purple blanket. Everything in the room had a familiar quality, but it was all still new.

A little frightened, I threw back the covers to check out what I looked like. I searched for my full-length mirror in the foreign bedroom, but it wasn't there, so I settled for a small mirror sitting on my desk. I inspected my face carefully to make sure I was still me. I was relieved to see the same Alexis looking back at me, but a second look at myself made me jump.

My eyes were… *glowing.* They were still deep blue, but now an eerie white light lined the rims of my pupils. The glow was so bright that I thought I might actually go blind if I looked at it for too long. Still, I couldn't stop staring at the strange white ring. It was fascinating yet frightening. It lit my eyes beautifully, but it had a scary, otherworldly quality.

Shocked, I dropped the glass mirror, where it shattered into sharp pieces that scattered across the hardwood floor. One shard cut my left foot, although I didn't feel the pain until I looked down and saw blood steadily dripping out.

I rushed out of the room and down the long, dark hallway, running at an incredible pace. I leaped down a set of stairs and dashed out of the house. Outside, instead of my beautiful forest, I saw only a few live oaks and a swimming pool.

Where was I? I felt completely confused and lost. All I could do was look around in bewilderment.

"Alexis," a smooth voice behind me said in relief. I spun around to see Taylor.

"Taylor?" I said, surprised. He was smiling at me and his eyes held a look of admiration, but I know my expression was one of doubt.

"You have no idea how badly I wanted to see you."

"Yeah, I'm sure I do," I said a bit sourly. His head cocked in confusion.

"I don't understand; I thought you'd be happy to see me."

"You know what, Taylor, I thought so, too, but after what I've been through, I think it would be best if you were not here."

Taylor paused before he replied: "Actually, after what you've been through, I think it's best that I am here." His tone grew more serious and his adoring expression melted.

"You don't know what you're talking about," I said harshly as I folded my arms and turned my back to him. In a fraction of a second, he stepped up close behind me.

"I know exactly what I'm talking about," he said sternly. "Alexis, you have to understand that what you have is a gift, and if you'd treat it like one, you could do great things." He sounded just like my mother. "But when you treat it like a curse," he continued, "it will destroy not only someone like Andy but also you."

At that moment, my head dropped, my hands covered my face, and I began to sob. He was in front of me in an instant. His strong arms wrapped around my body and drew me close to his. Taylor held me tightly for a long moment, but then, I pushed him away.

"What's wrong?" he asked, shocked at my behavior.

"You shouldn't be around me," I said darkly. "You could get hurt." He laughed, deep and throaty.

"I don't think that will be a problem now… seeing that this is a dream."

I looked up at him with tear-filled eyes. "What? This is a dream?"

He laughed again, a little louder this time.

"Well, yeah! What did you think was going on? Did you think you just magically flew to Florida?" His smile disintegrated.

"I'm in Florida? What?" Suddenly, a harsh gust of wind blew between us. I looked at him and he seemed frightened. He stared in the direction that the strange wind was coming from. I stared, as well.

A few yards away from us, a thick fog covered the yard, suddenly producing powerful gusts. The wind grew so loud that I had to shout over it to talk to Taylor.

"Taylor, what's going on? Tell me the truth!!" I was irritated by the fact that he was obviously trying to hide something.

"I can't, at least not now. But please, listen to me!" He grabbed both my shoulders firmly and looked me straight in the eye. "Everything is going to be okay. Trust me. Soon, everything that has happened to you will make sense; I'll be able to explain everything! Just be careful and think about what I said about your powers!" I was so lost in his words that all I could do was swallow hard and nod my head weakly. He looked in the direction of the wind again, seeming terrified.

"I will see you soon!" he shouted as the wind grew louder. He leaned in and kissed my forehead. "I promise!" With that, he ran off in the direction of the fog and wind.

Suddenly, as if someone had flipped a giant switch, the wind stopped. I couldn't make sense of what was happening. I stood in the strange backyard, lost in my own thoughts, as the scene grew darker and darker.

Jennifer

I laid in bed helplessly, playing Sudoku, sensing the anxiety emanating from Alexis's room. I tried to fight the powerful urge to go check on her by working on the puzzle in front of me. I had endured my share of bad situations in the past, but nothing was as difficult as being helpless in the face of my daughter's pain!

I glanced over at the clock on my bedside table. It was 3:00 in the morning, and I had been wide awake since Alexis started dreaming, around 10:00. I didn't think I could sleep, not when my child was in such emotional turmoil, but I put down my puzzle and tried.

I rubbed my eyes and laid my head down on the pillow. Closing my eyelids, I must have dozed off, but moments later, something made me jump.

I had heard someone. It wasn't Alexis or her thoughts.... It was someone else's thoughts, coming from her room. Frightened, I hustled out of my bedroom and into the dark hallway. I looked around carefully, searching for an intruder. The hall was clear. I dashed into Alexis's room to take a look.

Quickly but quietly, I threw open the door and peered into the darkness. I scanned the room as best I could without the lights on and without waking Alexis.

As I searched, my anxiety and adrenaline shot up even higher. My body was ready to defend my daughter. My mind raced through ridiculous worst-case scenarios. But no matter how silly your fears seem later, you can't help but believe them in a panicked state of mind.

The room was empty except for the sleeping Alexis, but at the same time, something seemed peculiar. I could've sworn I'd heard someone else. Never in my life had I been wrong about hearing the thoughts of another person.

"*Just relax, Jennifer…*," a voice in my mind said. "*You're getting upset over nothing. Both you and Alexis have had a long, hard day. You're just exhausted and hearing things.*" I had no idea where the words came from. I was uneasy at first, but then my tension subsided.

The random, spooky voice in my head had a point. I had dealt with a lot in just one day, and I was probably worn out. Maybe it would be best to go to bed and hope that things would seem better in the morning. I was definitely ready for some real sleep. But before leaving the room, I checked on Alexis again.

I knelt next to her bed, resting my folded arms on the edge of her mattress. I put my hand softly on her forehead. Her temperature was down, but she still felt warm, probably from all the nightmares she was having. As I stroked her hair, I felt that it was moist with sweat. Poor thing… she's having a rough night.

Before returning to my room, I tried one last time to look inside her head. I concentrated with all my might and power… but came up with nothing. The frustration was killing me. Every time I tried to get a quick glance inside her head, all I could see was fog. A thick, opaque, black fog. Usually when she was sleeping, her mind held a gentle emptiness, but this was different—and strange.

I finally decided that it was useless to try to figure out this new development when I was exhausted.

After a moment, I rose slowly from my knees and made my way to the door. As I walked down the dark hallway, I couldn't shake the feeling that someone was watching us… listening to us. I checked the house again but found no evidence that anything was wrong.

I climbed into bed and stared at the ceiling, wondering why I still couldn't fall asleep. My mind refused to shut down. Sometime later, I drifted off restlessly.

ଓ

I woke to the sunlight peeking through my white lace curtains. It created a glare on the mirror and bounced off my crystal lamp.

I slowly and lazily rose from my bed and made my way to the bathroom. I quickly ran a brush through my hair and brushed my teeth. Not bothering to change out of my pajamas, I pulled on the robe that hung from a hook on the bathroom wall.

I managed to drag myself into the kitchen and decided to make a good breakfast for Alexis.

Mechanically, I got out two pans, one large and one medium sized, and put a little bit of butter in the smaller one. I turned the heat up to medium on both burners and put several slices of bacon into the large pan. As that was cooking, I whisked two eggs in a bowl, then poured them into their pan. When breakfast was ready, I set the plate on the kitchen table and returned to the refrigerator to pour Alexis a glass of orange juice. I put the glass on the table next to the plate of hot food and stepped back to admire my workmanship. The meal looked and smelled terrific, which made me a bit hungry myself. I thought I'd settle for a bagel and tea after I woke up Alexis. Glancing at the clock, I was stunned to realize it was noon! I had no idea that I'd slept so late! Then it hit me that Alexis wasn't awake either, which was unusual. She had never even slept past 10:00 in her life! I was about to make my way toward her room when I heard a voice from outside.

I looked out the window to my left, where the sound seemed to be coming from. Ordinarily, I would assume it was another hiker nearby, but as I listened closer, I heard the deep voice from last night, and this time… there was more than one of them.

Immediately, I ran out the back door and onto the wooden deck. I looked around in front of me, listening attentively to where the thoughts were coming from. I picked up the strange voice coming from the east and took off after the source as fast as I could.

I was not as fast or as strong as Alexis, and after only a minute or two of running, I was already panting heavily and slowing in pace. But I pushed myself to keep going.

I could still hear the same two voices I'd been chasing, but suddenly, they seemed to come from different directions. I stopped and looked around, confused and desperate. The voice from last night seemed to come from the east and west at the same time. The second voice came from the north at first, then I heard it a second later in the south.

I didn't know which way to run. I started toward the west, but then I heard the voice coming from the south, so I changed my course. I would take a few steps in one direction, then have to turn in the other direction. I kept at it until, suddenly, the voices came to a halt.

I stopped in my tracks and fell to the ground. I was breathing heavily and panting from all the running I'd done. I pressed my hand against my forehead in a useless attempt to stop the pounding in my head. I had never had the experience of hearing two people's thoughts from different directions, and I didn't know why it was happening now. I desperately wanted to figure out what was going on, but after a few minutes of resting on the forest floor, I knew the answer wasn't going to come right then.

When the trees stopped spinning around me, I stood up and regained my balance, then made my way toward home. I hadn't realized how far I'd run until I reached the house and checked the clock in the kitchen. It was now a little past 12:30.

Wow. It certainly didn't feel like a half an hour when I was out there, but apparently, that's what it had been.

My thoughts returned to Alexis. I knew that she was probably exhausted from the day before, but still, she was not the type to waste half her day sleeping.

As I started down the hall to check on her, she walked sluggishly around the corner.

"Oh, you're awake," I said in relief.

"Yeah," she responded quietly.

"How are you feeling, honey?" I asked as I wrapped my arms around her and gave her a gentle squeeze.

"Tired," she answered. Her one-word responses were starting to worry me again. She sounded and looked like she was in rough shape. Her face was blank and emotionless. Her eyes seemed to be locked on the floor, as if she was trying to find her answers in the deep-colored wood. She had dark circles under her eyes and her body was slumped. When she spoke, her voice was hoarse and raspy. She didn't even hug me back when I hugged her. Her arms stayed by her side and her eyes remained empty.

"Well, I made you some breakfast," I said, trying to sound cheerful. "But I'm sure it's cold by now. How about a sausage, egg, and cheese biscuit? It's one of your favorites." I waited for a response as she continued to look at the floor.

"No, thanks," she finally said, then walked past me without even a moment of eye contact.

"Are you sure, hon? You haven't eaten anything for almost twenty-four hours. It would make you feel better," I encouraged.

"Yeah, like a biscuit is going to make all my problems go away," Alexis said, with her back toward me. I was surprised by her tone. Instead of her usual bratty sarcasm, her words sounded dark and sad.

"Um, I meant it would perk you up a bit. When you don't eat, your body becomes exhausted and so does your mind."

"I'll eat later," she promised. I was troubled by Alexis's behavior, but I told myself that it was probably best to let her eat when she was ready.

"All right, honey, just let me know when you want something."

"Okay." She was making her way back to her room when I stopped her.

"Alexis?" She turned slowly to look at me, but this time, I didn't try to make eye contact. I was afraid of what I would see. "Whenever you're ready to talk, I'll be ready to listen," I said.

"Thanks, Mom." As she spoke, I saw her mouth twitch for half a second. Seeing her attempt at a smile, I couldn't help but smile myself.

But when she turned to walk back to her room, I saw a tear escape from her left eye, and my smile vanished immediately.

A few seconds later, I heard the sound of her door closing quietly, and I listened as she began to cry. I sat down at the table, and my own tears plopped onto the cold food.

This situation was killing me. It was bad enough that I couldn't hear anything going on in my daughter's head, but the fact that there was nothing I could do to help her pushed me over the edge. I wept silently as I listened to my broken daughter's violent sobbing from the other side of the quiet house.

Alexis

Chapter 7

Why was all this weird stuff happening to me? Up until the accident at school, I had been a pretty good person. Endowed with some strange powers—yes—and maybe a little antisocial, but I hadn't ever done anything terrible. Why was I being punished? I felt that some big cosmic force must really hate me to put me through this torture.

Not only was I being tortured, but I couldn't even begin to imagine the pain Andy's family was going through. Just thinking about a worried mother at her son's hospital bedside brought on waves of tears. How could I have hurt Andy? I was such a monster. Knowing that the whole thing could have easily been avoided made it worse. All it would have taken to save Andy was for me to run out of the classroom. But I hadn't done that. My actions were irreversible. No matter how far away or how many times mom and I moved, there was no escaping what I had done. The memory of that day would haunt me forever.

I lay on my back, staring at the bare ceiling and drowning in despair. I knew I was pathetic and I knew I was being selfish by sharing my misery with my mother, but I couldn't help it. It felt as if someone had ripped out my heart, taken off with it, and hadn't even bothered to turn back around to see the gaping hole in my chest.

I turned on my side as I let out a heavy, tired yawn. I closed my eyes for a brief second to rest them, but moments later, I drifted into sleep.

ଔଔଔ

The next thing I knew, someone was shaking me awake. At first, I refused to be stirred, but whoever wanted me to get up was very impatient.

"OW!" I shouted angrily. I felt a nip at my ankle, as if I had been bitten by a puppy. I sat up immediately and looked around. When I did, I met the eyes of a curious little coyote.

He sat innocently on his hind end and stared at me with his ears pricked forward. He wasn't very big, which made me guess he was still young. He had bright, playful blue eyes and sand-colored fur. As I continued to stare, it seemed as if he was examining me, as well. He cocked his head from side to side and occasionally sniffed in my direction. I smiled at him and I could have sworn I saw him smile back.

Okay, this was getting out of hand. The last thing I remember was crying in my room; now, I seemed to be outside again.

I got up from the wet ground and took a good look around. I was surrounded by beautiful trees and fresh flowers. It looked like my forest except that this one was untouched by my violence. There was wildlife everywhere! I turned around and saw a rabbit munching on a branch. I looked to my left and saw a mother doe and her fawn gazing at me cautiously. Multicolored flowers sprouted up from the ground and multicolored birds perched in the trees. The sunlight peeked through the thick leaves in a way that lit up the forest perfectly. My smile grew as my glance darted around the picturesque scene.

Soon enough, the little troublemaker who had woken me up tugged on the leg of my jeans. I looked down and met his lighthearted eyes. He instantly let go of my pants and started jumping and prancing around like a puppy.

I think the little guy was looking for a friend and saw me as a good candidate. I looked around for a toy for him to play with. I picked up a stick that was lying next to my right foot, showed it to him, then flung it away from me. The piece of rotting wood flew like lightning through the tranquil forest, and the coyote ran after it. He was gone in a flash but didn't come back as quickly as he left.

After several minutes, I figured the stick must have landed in a bush, and the coyote was having trouble finding it. I thought about going to help him, but why spoil his fun? In the meantime, I continued to admire the beauty of the forest.

I sat down on the leafy, damp floor and took in the harmony around me. A large purple flower grew next to me, and I uprooted it from the soil. Closing my eyes, I inhaled its heavenly aroma. But when I slowly opened my eyes again, I found that the warm, bright weather had turned dark and cold.

What the hell?

The ground where I was sitting was covered with a heavy blanket of snow. I got up and stared in amazement. As I stood in the clearing, dumbfounded, I heard a cry in the distance. I instantly knew who needed my help.

Without hesitating, I sprinted in the direction of the yelp. As I ran, I had the sensation of being followed. The events of the past couple of days had made me a paranoid freak, so I glanced over my shoulder to check. Behind me was not a person or an animal but a trail. A narrow, jet-black path covered my every step. The appearance of the trail made me nervous, but another yelp in the distance drove me forward.

Several questions raced through my mind: *Where am I, and why am I here? Why do I keep having all these weird dreams, and what do they mean?* I wanted to stop and try to figure things out, but I had a feeling my new little friend needed me.

I arrived at a perfectly round meadow. The trees that lined the perimeter almost looked as if they were protecting this place. I stood on the outskirts of a ring of giant trees and peeked into the meadow. As I scanned the field, I saw my furry little troublemaker. He was looking around anxiously and desperately, as if he couldn't find his way out of the meadow. I smiled when I saw that he was okay, but I knew by the strange atmosphere and the wild look in his eye that the situation was becoming dangerous.

I took a step toward the coyote to call him to me before something went wrong, but just then, someone else entered the scene.

A young woman with traditional Native American clothing and a thick animal-fur coat strolled into the snow-covered field. I couldn't see her face, but I knew she was a girl by the way she walked and by her feminine figure. Her worn moccasins made deep footprints in the untouched snow as she sauntered toward my coyote.

She stopped a few feet in front of the little guy and stared down at him. One dark hand stayed at her side as she reached behind herself to grip the bow that hung from her back. Coyote let out a few whimpers and tried to sink himself deeper into the ground. My hand came to my mouth to keep myself from crying out as the young woman, with her back still toward me, reached for her long tube filled with multicolored arrows.

Tears fell from my eyes and my left hand gripped a tree with tremendous force. I wanted to run into the meadow and protect the pup, but my stubborn legs wouldn't allow it. I was completely paralyzed from the waist down.

The young woman now had her bow and arrow aimed at the little coyote. He lowered his head and tightly closed his eyes, as if accepting defeat. She slowly pulled back the string of her weapon, then carefully and accurately released it.

My innocent friend fell into the snow silently, where he would never rise again.

"No," I breathed quietly. The young Native American jerked her gaze away from the coyote and slowly scanned the field. She had heard me and had her bow tightly gripped, ready to be used. She turned her body in the direction of the tree that hid me. I held my breath, fearful that she would see me as she searched the trees. After a long moment, she turned her back to me and stared intently at my blood-stained friend.

My body trembled with pure anger. Without a second thought, I leaped out from behind the tree and roared, "I'M OVER HERE, YOU SADISTIC COWARD!" I waited for her to turn around and face me, but she didn't. She continued to gawk at the coyote, as if taking pride in what she had done.

When she didn't respond, I sprinted toward the middle of the field where she stood. In a flash—literally—I was standing directly behind her. Without thinking, I grabbed her by the shoulder and spun her around so that I could see her face. As she turned, the furry dark hood that had concealed her features fell away. My hand dropped to my side as my rage dissolved and terror washed over me.

I knew her. The young, tanned, sadistic coward was… me. She had my exact facial features: the almond shape of my eyes, the skinny bridge of my nose, and even the widow's peak at the top of my forehead. Every feature was the same except that this young woman had darker skin, brown eyes, and black hair. I studied her in fright as she stood, gazing at me without emotion, as if she was made of metal.

Suddenly, her dark skin began to fade to my exact skin tone right before my eyes. Then, her hair morphed from jet black to dark brunette. Her eyes, which had been brown, turned completely black, with a burning green ring in the middle. Her expression abruptly changed from detachment to rage, as if she had just noticed that I was standing in front of her.

My eyes grew wild with fear as hers did with wrath. I turned to run, but she had a hold of me before I even took a step forward. She roughly whirled me around to meet her deadly stare. After a moment, she gripped my shoulders and lifted me from the ground, then heaved me at least a hundred yards across the meadow. I screamed as I flew, then crashed into a tree with a flash of light.

ଓଓଓ

Despite the fact that the whole experience was just a dream, I couldn't help but jump and cry out when my body hit the tree. Now that I was awake, I felt like an idiot.

I sat upright and ran my fingers through my unruly hair. I wiped the sweat from my forehead and let out a deep, slow sigh. After a minute, I gathered my thoughts.

Like anybody, when I have a nightmare, I usually wake up out of breath, with my heart pounding. But this time was different; I was… *okay.* Sadly, I had almost forgotten what okay felt like. In fact, I was intrigued by the dream.

Could it contain some sort of message? Maybe it was meant to be… a sign or a warning. I wasn't sure how, but somehow I knew it had meaning; I just hadn't put the pieces together yet.

As I was thinking, I heard a gentle knock at my door. My mother came in with a plate of food.

"Hey, Lex, I made you something to eat. Are you hungry?" she asked in a soft voice.

My stomach managed to answer her before I did.

"Yeah, thanks, Mom," I said as I attempted a half smile. I took the plate from her hands and set it on my lap. I was trying to work up the courage to ask my mother something I had been curious about for a long time. "Um, Mom?" I began.

"Yes?" she answered.

"Well, I sort of… if you don't mind, I wanted to… talk about something." I played with the chips on the plate as I spoke, not daring to meet her gaze.

"Of course, we can." I looked up at her relieved expression and her caring eyes and smiled. She sat next to my feet on the edge of the bed and settled herself.

"There are some things I've always wondered about."

"Like?" my mother pressed.

"Well, like... us," I tried to explain. There was a pause before my mother spoke again.

"What exactly do you want to know?" she asked coolly. I took in a quick breath before starting.

"How did we get our special powers?" I asked timidly. My mother paused to think, then inhaled deeply.

"To be honest, honey, I don't really know," she said. "I think it's mostly just genetics, you know, like how people inherit their hair color or eye color. I think the same thing applies to our powers."

I thought about her explanation for a moment before responding. "I guess that makes sense. But if we were to somehow trace our ancestors all the way back to the very beginning, to the first people on earth, how did they inherit their powers?" I asked.

My mother was quick to respond. "I don't know. They've just been... around. Nobody has ever questioned them..."

"But there has to be some history behind our powers. I mean, our ancestors didn't just magically have powers all of a sudden. They had to come from somewhere, right?"

"Hon, I wish I knew more, but I don't," Mom said gently. "All I know is that somewhere on my side of the family, some of our ancestors were of Native American descent. Maybe that's part of the answer."

I felt my eyes grow wide as my heart pounded against my rib cage. Holy crap… was that why I had that dream?

Before I could ask any more questions, my mom changed the subject: "Why don't you finish your sandwich and then maybe afterwards, you and I could go for a walk," she suggested. I really didn't have the energy to get up and move, but I knew it would be better if I did.

"Okay."

"Great, let me know when you want to go." She rose from my bed and walked toward the door. Suddenly, I felt awful again. The back of my throat closed up and I had to blink back tears. As soon as the door was closed, I began to cry.

Thoughts of the accident at school rushed into my mind, as if someone had blown the dam that kept the dark emotions from flooding my psyche. I thought I was okay there for a minute, but I knew that after what I'd done to Andy, I'd never really be okay again. I hoped and prayed that *he* would.

"Why?" I whispered fiercely as my head fell back on my pillow. "WHY?! Why are you doing this to me?!" I wasn't sure who I was speaking to, but something had to take the blame for what I was going through, and it might as well be the ceiling. "Damn this curse! UGH!!! I hate this! My stupid powers are the reason Andy is in a coma! Why can't I just be NORMAL?!" I was close to shouting with intense emotion.

Suddenly, I heard a voice speaking to me from inside: "*Alexis, relax! The only reason you're feeling this way is because you haven't fully faced what happened at school. If you just....*" The voice trailed off and became nothing but a whisper.

I shook my head, trying not to listen to... whoever was talking to me. *I must be losing my mind*, I thought. The voice sounded familiar, but it was too faint for me to figure out exactly who it belonged to.

After a few minutes, I finally settled down. I wasn't okay, but at least I wasn't hysterical.

I got up stiffly out of bed and changed into a comfortable T-shirt and a pair of shorts. My body felt numb, like a hand or a foot that had fallen asleep, and my eyes were sore from crying. I threw my knotted hair into a pony tail and grabbed a comfortable pair of sneakers. Just as I was tying my shoes, I heard my mother call from down the hall.

"Alexis, are you ready?" she asked.

I shouted back without thinking: "Ugh... HOLD ON, MOM! Just give me ONE MINUTE!" I really didn't mean to be so touchy and disrespectful. I guess it was official; I had lost my sanity.

"Calm down!!" she yelled back impatiently. I couldn't blame her for being mad at me. I had probably used up every ounce of patience she had left.

I walked out of my room and down the hallway. I rounded the corner and saw my mother at the front door, with her hand on the doorknob. When she turned to look at me, I dropped my head in shame and guilt.

"I'm sorry, Mom. I really didn't mean to talk to you like that," I apologized in a choked and quiet tone. I heard her take a deep breath before responding.

"I know. Just promise me you'll try to do a better job of controlling yourself." She shut her eyes as if that would make what she said a little less harsh. But her words were still impatient and stern, which made them painful to listen to. Of course, I didn't tell her that.

"I'll try," I said as I slowly lifted my heavy gaze up from the floor. She nodded her head and turned the cold golden knob in front of her.

Chapter 8

The forest seemed composed—not very lively but generally at ease. The trees stood still as the occasional breeze fluttered by. The sky was dreary and overcast, and the air was filled with the subtle scent of stale maple leaves. The light, rocky soil was hard and cold as my mother and I walked over it.

My body was stiff and tired because I had been in bed for two straight days. My eyes were still sore and dry from crying, and my energy was completely zapped. I felt like one of the walking dead I had once seen in a zombie movie.

My mother and I walked for a while before either of us spoke. Finally, she asked cautiously, "So, why are you suddenly so interested in our family's history?"

"It's just, I think it's something I should know about."

There was a short pause before Mom said, "Okay, well, I don't know much about where our powers originated. But I do know some other stuff you might be interested in, like what my family was like."

"Spill it," I said.

My mother paused before speaking. "Let's see, where should I start? Umm... your grandmother, my mother, has powers similar to mine, except not as strong or complex."

Before my mother continued, I interrupted with another question. "Why aren't her powers as strong as yours?"

"You see, in my mother and father's generation, they were the most powerful people of their kind. They both had psychological powers, so when they had me, I got a double dose, so to speak."

I took a minute to digest what she had said before responding. "Okay, that seems logical." As I spoke, I was thinking of something else. If my mother had psychological powers and I had physical powers, then my worst fears were confirmed. I had inherited my strength from someone just as dangerous as me. I wanted to know why I didn't get her powers instead of this mystery man's, but I didn't want to make my fear obvious, so I tried wording my question in a way that wouldn't tip my mother off. "But what if two people with different types of powers have a kid—how does that work?" Despite my efforts, I think my mother caught on to what I was really asking, but she didn't want to bring up my father either.

"That's where God comes in. In that type of situation, you can't guarantee which power the child will inherit. But how strong the child's power is still depends on how powerful the parents are."

I was starting to understand my life a little better as my mother spoke, but I still needed more information. "So basically, each generation gets more powerful?"

"Exactly, but one family may not start out as powerful as another. Like I said, it depends on how powerful the parents are."

After a moment of silence, I thought of a question that—oddly—had never occurred to me before. "Are there any more families like us?" I asked. My mother's face tensed subtlety.

"Of course, there aren't. What would give you that idea?" Her voice sounded flat and stressed.

"Oh, it's just that… it seemed like that's what you were saying." She looked to the ground, and her body tightened as she listened to me.

"I was just speaking hypothetically, honey. Nothing real, just hypothetical." My mom's explanation made no sense. I wanted to know if she was hiding something, but it seemed best not to pursue the subject.

Mom walked forward, still looking at the ground, deeper into the woods. There was a long, awkward silence before I spoke again.

"What about grandpa; what kind of powers does he have?" I asked to break the tension. It seemed to work.

"Ah, now, that's an interesting subject." She smiled when she spoke, but it wasn't a happy smile, more sarcastic than anything else. She rolled her eyes a bit before continuing. "Grandpa is a complicated character. He's actually a person of mixed powers. He bears both the power of mind reading, from his father, and the power of strength, from his mother. It's extremely rare for two different abilities to be combined in one person, but with Grandpa, it just happened." She looked preoccupied, as if she was trying to figure out the strange case of Grandpa.

"I never knew that. I never knew any of this. How come we've never talked about it?" I asked.

"I guess I've been waiting for the right time to explain it all," Mom answered flatly. I nodded my head with understanding.

My mom was smart to wait. Our lives were pretty complicated, and it didn't surprise me that there was a lot I didn't know. I wouldn't have been shocked to learn that there was more to our family history, but I hoped there weren't any more secrets.

"You know," Mom began, "your father's side of the family has some interesting people, too."

I looked away from her and spoke tensely. "I don't care."

"Alexis, even though your father is gone, he's still a part of you. Nothing is going to change that. If you're trying to understand your powers better, you need to know about both halves of yourself."

"What's there to understand? My powers are dangerous and better off ignored—along with my so-called father. I was just curious about our heritage. I don't want to talk about that man or my curse."

My mom was obviously disturbed by my erratic behavior, but she decided to leave the matter alone.

As we continued our walk, my mother and I heard a noise that made us stop in our tracks.

"Did you hear that?" I asked in a hushed tone.

"Yeah, it's coming from those bushes." She moved her head in the direction she was referring to. We listened as what sounded like the footsteps of a huge creature crunched thin, dry twigs and ruffled the leaves close to the ground. A closer look into the bushes revealed the golden brown eyes of a hunter peeking through the vegetation.

"Mom, you need to get out of here," I said sternly. She, too, saw what was lurking in the brush.

"There's no time," she whispered. "It'll catch me if I try to run. Besides, I'm not leaving you here alone with that." The golden brown eyes moved closer to the ground. The creature was poised to pounce at any moment.

"Mom, I've dealt with these things before; I'll be fine. But if you're here and the cat doesn't get to you first, I might turn on you after the fight," I said quickly and quietly.

"Don't worry; I'll hide, and the second you get rid of that thing,

I'll calm you down." There wasn't enough time for us to argue, so I reluctantly agreed.

"Fine, just stay behind that tree over there and away from me." She nodded her head as I turned back to fight the panther, but then she made a mistake. She took off as fast as she could to the tree I had told her to hide behind. I knew that panthers are attracted to fast movement and will chase anything running away from them.

"NO!! DON'T—" I shouted, but my sentence was cut off as the giant mountain cat leaped onto my back and knocked me to the ground.

I heard the tremendous roar of the panther and the faint cry of my mother. With all my might and power, I managed to make my voice heard over the cat. "GO! GO TO THE TREE NOW!!!" I couldn't see if she obeyed my orders, but I thought I heard her footsteps recede.

I reached over my shoulder, grabbed the panther by the neck, and flipped it over on its back. I pushed myself up off the ground weakly and tentatively touched the deep gashes and claw marks on my upper back. When I brought my hand in front of my face, my fingers were covered in crimson.

There was no way in hell that I could run away from the panther with my injuries slowing me down; even with my speed, it would catch me in a heartbeat. My only chance was to fight.

I drew in a deep breath as the massive cat rose slowly to its feet and crouched. A deep, sinister growl emerged from its throat. It almost sounded as if it was laughing at me, and I grew angry.

Suddenly, a sense of strength and rejuvenation washed over me. I felt energetic and focused. As far as I was concerned, this cat had pounced on its last mouse.

The panther lunged toward me, but I grabbed its outstretched paws and tossed it into a tree—not the one my mother was hiding behind. The cat quickly rose to its feet. I ran toward it with incredible speed, ready to finish the fight, but its mighty jaws clamped down on my upper arm. It held my triceps tightly while I kicked it as hard as I could in the gut. The panther let out a wail of agony and released my arm.

I felt no pain anywhere, although for most people, my injuries might have been fatal. Adrenaline rushed through my veins and my heart pounded with exhilaration, but strangely, I also felt in complete control. My thoughts weren't clouded with rage like they usually were; this time, my mind was clear and determined.

The cat rose slowly from the ground and glared at me with eyes of defeat and desire for revenge. I was sure it wanted to rip me to shreds but was too hurt.

It was weird that I didn't go after the panther again at that moment. I know myself well enough to know that usually in a situation like this, that cat would be dead in a few seconds. But this time, I didn't feel compelled to kill. Somehow, I had a choice; I wasn't a slave to my curse.

It didn't have control of me like it did when the accident happened at school.

The panther and I stared at each other for a long moment before it slowly limped away, disappearing into the woods. Once the cat was out of sight, the pain kicked in, but it was nothing I couldn't stand.

My mother came out from hiding behind the tree a few seconds later. I expected her to run and hug me, but she stood beside the tree, wide-eyed in disbelief.

"Alexis," she said quietly. I felt my glow of triumph fade as panic returned. I hoped she hadn't been terrified by my actions.

"Mom, I know that was scary to watch, and I'm sorry you had to see it." I walked carefully toward her, and she reluctantly came forward, as well.

"Honey, we've got to get you home. Right now," she said with anxiety.

"The cuts don't hurt as bad as they look. It's nothing to freak out about," I lied, trying to reassure her, but she continued to stare. "Why are you looking at me like that?" I asked, a bit annoyed.

"Trust me, Lex, we definitely have something to freak out about right now," she said. The anxiety in her voice made me nervous. I obeyed her orders and followed her quickly back to the house.

☙

My mother opened the front door forcefully and walked straight back to her bedroom. I trailed close behind. As I followed her into the bathroom, I still didn't know what she was so worried about.

"Mom, when are going to tell me what's wrong?" I asked with a mixture of annoyance and anxiety.

"I was hoping *you* could explain it to *me*," she said, bewildered, as she gestured to the mirror on the wall next to her.

"What exactly is… *it*?" I asked, nervous. My mom didn't answer my question. Instead, she took a step back so that I could see what she was talking about.

"Oh. My. Gosh," I whispered. What I saw in the mirror made me forget all about the bleeding wounds on my arm and back.

"I don't know what it is," my mother began. "I've never seen anything like it." There was a short moment of silence before I spoke.

"But I have," I said stiffly as I stared at the familiar light burning in my eyes.

☙

"Alexis? Are you still with me?" I heard my mother say.

"Mhm" was my only response. I was almost completely blacked out. I could hear her, barely, and I could mumble a little bit, but other than that, I was hardly conscious.

My mother had been assessing my wounds as I lay limply on her bed. Now, she scooped me into her arms and started to carry me.

"C'mon," she said, "we need help. Now." I allowed her put me in the car, and a moment later, I felt the vehicle begin to move.

After a short ride, hands reached into the car to pull me out. I was lifted from the back seat to what I assumed to be a stretcher.

"What happened?" a strong, masculine voice said.

"Panther attack in the woods," my mother answered from right next to me. She held my hand as the stretcher began to move.

"We need to get her to the emergency room stat," another masculine voice said.

"Right," answered the man who had lifted me onto the stretcher.

"No!" my mother exclaimed. "You have to call Dr. Seymour; he's the only one she sees."

"I'm sorry, but Dr. Seymour isn't at the hospital today and couldn't get here for at least an hour. Your daughter needs immediate care and…." Before the second man could finish his sentence, my mother cut him off.

"Listen here, Mr. Paramedic," my mother said through gritted teeth, "you better believe she needs immediate care, but the only doctor she sees is Dr. Seymour." Her voice was dangerously quiet, and I was sure she was ready to rip the guy's head off.

"Ma'am," the paramedic said slowly, as if he was speaking to a child, "I'm sure if we called Dr. Seymour, he'd tell you the same thing. There are other doctors here at the hospital who can help your daughter." His tone was patronizing, which I knew would spark the look of death in Mom's eyes.

"Oh, is that so?" she asked sarcastically. "I suggest you do call Dr. Seymour and tell him who's here. Then maybe we'll all see if he'll come." She spoke with an uncomfortable sweetness in her voice, as if she were taunting the paramedic, which she probably was.

The men let out an irritated sigh before one of them spoke: "Okay, lady, but I'm not making any promises," he warned.

Sure enough, just a few moments after I had been wheeled into a treatment room, a nurse appeared to tell my mother that I would be stitched up by Dr. Seymour.

The nurse left us in a cold, quiet room. The air conditioning felt good on my sore muscles and wounds. I felt myself drifting off to sleep as my mother paced. The last thing I remember as I dozed was the sound of Dr. Seymour's calm and quiet voice.

☙

In the distance, voices were growing closer. One was my mother's—that I was sure of—but there were a few that were not familiar.

"When do you think she'll wake up?" my mother asked. Her voice was so quiet that I was surprised she could be heard.

"It shouldn't be too long now, Ms. Randall. Dr. Seymour will come back and check on her in a few minutes. In the meantime, try talking to her. That will probably wake her up a little quicker," an elderly voice replied.

"Thanks," my mother said appreciatively. I heard soft footsteps walk out of the room and the sound of my mother sitting down in a chair next to me.

"Alexis, if you can hear me honey, try to wake up. We need to make sure you're okay." I felt too weak to answer at first, but after a moment, I sensed that my mother was crying. I forced my eyes open and strained to turn my head and face her.

"Hi," I managed to say in a thick, raspy voice. Mom lifted her red eyes to mine. It seemed that I had just lifted a two hundred–pound weight off her back.

"Oh, honey!" she said with relief. "I'm so happy to hear your voice!" She put her hand on my cheek and kissed my forehead.

"Calm down, Mom. I'm fine; I just fell asleep for an hour or so. No biggie." My mother looked at me in astonishment. "What?" I asked.

"Lex, you've been out for five days." The moment she spoke, panic rippled through me.

"What? How is that possible?" I asked in disbelief.

"I'm sure I'll be able to explain," a familiar, soft voice said from the doorway. Both my mother and I met the hazel-colored eyes of Dr. Seymour. He came to the edge of my bed and took the clipboard that was attached to the railing.

"Alexis, when you got here, you had already lost a lot of blood, and you were slowly slipping into a coma. Luckily, I got here quickly and was able sew you up without being kicked into the wall or having your mother have to go to the trouble of mind-wiping you." Dr. Seymour followed his words with a grin and a wink.

Yeah, you heard right. He knows.

I was twelve when we first moved to Tennessee, and I needed an annual checkup to get into school. As it turned out, my mother had failed to mention that I had to get a tetanus shot so that I could register for seventh grade. I'm deathly afraid of needles, so it's not hard to imagine how well that turned out. Let's just say I was surprised that Dr. Seymour didn't file a lawsuit… or get killed, for that matter. My mother managed to charm him into keeping our secret, and I swore that I'd put on my big girl pants if I ever had to get another shot.

"After we got you stitched and cleaned up," Dr. Seymour continued, "I took some x-rays and found several broken ribs and a few shattered bones in your arm."

I looked down to see that I had a temporary cast on one arm, the same one that the panther had chomped down on. Dr. Seymour continued to catalog the injuries on my body.

"One of your ribs was close to puncturing you lung, but thankfully, it missed by a centimeter or two. You also slipped into a light coma, which is why you feel like you've been asleep for only a few hours. But we're certainly glad to see you looking a little more responsive now." I took a minute to process all this information.

"Wow, that's all?" I asked sarcastically as I tried to sit up straight and stretch my stiff body parts. But before I could move, Dr. Seymour stopped me.

"Oh, hey, I wouldn't do that! Did you not hear me just say *broken ribs* and *a shattered arm*?" he exclaimed with a hint of panic in his voice.

"Don't worry, Kent, she's fine. Just watch," my mother reassured him. They both turned to see me climb out of bed, stretch, walk across the room, and crawl back into bed with no problems at all. The doctor's eyes opened wide and his mouth hung open.

"What… how? Her injuries were very serious; she shouldn't be able to do that, not without stumbling in pain at least!" he said in bewilderment. My mother and I exchanged a look that seemed to say, *Do you want to tell him or should I?*

"Let's just say… she's a fast healer," my mother said playfully.

Dr. Seymour let out a short huff of breath and shook his head in amazement. "You Randalls never cease to amaze me." His eyes locked on to my mother's for a moment before I interrupted.

"So when can I get out of this joint?" I asked. I was sort of joking, but at the same time, I really wanted to jump out of bed and get away from the hospital.

"Let's get at least one more x-ray just to be sure. But if everything checks out, I don't see why you couldn't be home by this evening," Dr. Seymour said, still looking a little skeptical.

"Thanks, Kent," my mother responded.

Call me crazy, but her eyes seemed a little too dreamy for my liking.

"Yeah, thanks," I said with sudden hostility. Dr. Seymour didn't seem to notice my change of tone, but I knew who did. Mom shot me the classic death glare most mothers give their kids when they do something bad. Her expression spoke volumes: *I heard that, but you better hope he didn't!* Not surprisingly, I felt about three inches tall.

"All right, then," Dr. Seymour said after an awkward pause. "I'll send a nurse to take you for the x-ray in just a few minutes. If everything looks okay, I'll sign your release papers. " With that, he turned and walked swiftly out the door, closing it behind him. I really wished he hadn't left.

"What was that?!" my mother roared.

"What was what?" I asked in an irritated tone.

"You know very well what! You *never* disrespect an adult like that, *ever*, especially not Dr. Seymour!"

When she spoke those last words, my blood boiled as if poison was shooting through my veins. I felt a burning sensation all over my body.

"What do you mean by 'especially Dr. Seymour'?" I asked in a sarcastic sing-song.

For a split second, fear seemed to flash in my mother's eyes, but her face remained cold and hard. After a moment, she said, "I just mean that he's done a lot for us; you should be grateful to him."

"Hah! For what?" I asked mockingly. My tone made my mother even angrier than I was, and trust me, that's a really bad thing.

"Um, well, let's see...," my mother began sarcastically. "How about all the medical records he has to falsify to keep others from growing suspicious about us and all the sacrifices he's made for us. He drove here on his day off when I first brought you to the emergency room, and he's been in to see you three or four times a day while you were unconscious. Every time you're sick, he comes to our house to take care of you. And you know what? I never asked him to do any of that. He puts his own career in danger because he cares about us and our safety. Did you ever think of any of that? Huh? How selfish can you be?" Her last words sounded so bleak and cold that my rage dissipated and my stomach sank.

I didn't know what to think. My eyes blinked back tears of anguish, my throat blocked the way for angry words to come spewing out, and my muscles refused to let me run away. All I could do was stare at my mother. In return, she looked mortified, as if she hadn't realized the depth of her own emotions. She opened her mouth to speak, but we were interrupted.

"Excuse me." The elderly nurse whom I had heard earlier was standing in the doorway.

Her face was marked by soft, leathery wrinkles and many spots of sun damage. Her eyes were wise and clear, stormy gray in color, and her hair was thinning and white, but her voice was smooth and elegant.

"Am I interrupting?" she asked gently. I shifted my gaze from the nurse back to my mother, shooting her a cold, hard look that would have sent shivers down my own spine if I had looked into a mirror.

"No, not at all," I finally spoke. "In fact, we were just about through." My mother's face held the same look of mortification as I continued to stare.

"Very well. I'm here to take you to x-ray." The nurse helped me into a wheelchair and steered us out the door. As I was wheeled away, I shot my mother another cold, expressionless stare.

Chapter 9

The tension between my mother and me was bone crushing. My stomach felt like it was in knots, and each time I took a breath, my chest hurt. I kept my shaky hands busy by playing a game on my phone, trying to divert myself from the idea of punching someone in the face.

My mother kept her tight eyes on the road ahead of us while her anxious fingers tapped at the steering wheel. I could tell the heavy atmosphere was getting to her as well, but unfortunately, we both share a similar fatal flaw: We are too proud for our own good. To her, speaking first would be like saying, "I was wrong and you were right." To me, launching a conversation would show weakness, and I can never be weak, ever. It is simply not an option.

Every few minutes, I would get tired of my phone and stare out the window. We were on an interstate, so there wasn't really much to look at, just a lot of cars and a few big trucks.

After a long moment, I heard Mom ask: "Alexis? What are you staring at?"

"Oh, um… it's nothing," I replied in a hard, quiet tone. Hearing my mother speak made me remember how angry I was at her. As I thought about our fight, my body tensed. My hands shook and balled into fists. I knew where this situation was going: downhill… and fast.

I began to panic, thinking about what would happen if my mother didn't control me in time. At the same time, my anger was feeding me nonsense, telling me, *She deserves whatever she has coming.* I tried to shake the thoughts away, but they were too powerful. I managed to blurt out a warning.

"Mom, pull over!" I screamed. She looked at me like I had completely lost my mind (which I was going to in about thirty seconds).

"Alexis, what in the world?!" she spat furiously. I was still fighting with my anger, but I wouldn't be able to hold it off much longer.

"Either pull over or control me. QUICK!" I said in a strained voice. I was sweating and shaking uncontrollably. I had my eyes squeezed tightly shut in an attempt to ward off the pain. Trying to control my powers is not only exhausting, but it's also unbearably painful. Resisting the curse is like being run over by a truck… repeatedly.

"Honey, I– I can't. I have no control over you! I'll pull over; just hang in there!" Mom said. She tried to sound calm, but I could tell she was freaking out.

"OHH!!! HUURRRRYYYY!!!" I wailed at the top of my lungs.

Fortunately, there wasn't much traffic, so my mom gunned the engine, flying through the exit and skidding to a stop at the edge of the road. She *finally* understood what was happening and tried frantically to calm me down.

"Okay. Home isn't far from here. Just take this street all the way down until– " My cries of pain cut her off.

"AHH... SHORT VERSION, PLEASE!" I barked in frustration. Mom reached into the glove compartment and grabbed a map.

"Here, this will help. Be safe… I love you." A tiny bit of pain melted away when she said that, but it wasn't enough. I tried to give her a reassuring look, but when her eyes met mine, she gasped and nearly jumped through the car roof. She stared at me in pure terror.

Immediately, fresh pain came rushing back. Before it was too late, I threw the door open and ran as fast as possible toward the woods. I didn't care if anyone saw me. I would be out of the state faster than a passing driver could say, "What the hell was that?"

଒

I don't know how long I ran into the woods, probably no more than two or three hours. I'd stop every now and then to punch a tree or lift one up from its roots, then throw it a mile or two across the forest… the usual way for me to deal with my anger. After a while, I started to think that I might have run a little too far away from home.

I remembered the map my mother had given me and pulled it out of my back pocket. I tried to read it, but it was useless given that I was in the middle of a forest with no compass and no sense of where I was. I threw the map on the ground and pulled out my phone. I knew there had to be an application for a GPS.

"Thank God for technology," I said, before looking at my signal strength. Of course... no bars. Just my luck. I decided to walk around until I got a signal.

After about twenty minutes of aimless wandering, I heard the sound of cars in the distance. Finally, some good news! I ran for the source of the sound. A few short seconds later, I was next to a highway. I looked around for a sign and was shocked at what I found. So much for good news.

According to the helpful sign, if I kept traveling in the same direction for fifty-eight more miles, I would be in Richmond... as in VIRGINIA!

"You've GOT to be kidding me," I said aloud in frustration. I stood rooted by the side of the highway, amazed at the fact that I had just run more than five hundred miles without becoming even remotely tired. It's crazy how much power I get from that stupid curse.

I gathered my thoughts and opened up the GPS application on my phone. I typed in my location—Richmond—and punched in where I was trying to go, which was Chattanooga. After a few seconds, a little map with a highlighted route popped up on my phone. Without hesitation, I dashed back into the woods, following the edge of the highway in the direction of home.

☙

After a couple of hours, I was behind my house, but I stayed hidden in the trees, unable to bring myself to go inside.

What was I going to tell my mother? What did she see before I ran off that freaked her out so much (besides the fact that I was about to obliterate her)? Should I tell her about my dreams? Should I tell her what *really* happened in the forest the other week—when I blacked out? I didn't know how much I wanted to share with her. Finally, I swallowed hard and walked up to the back door of my dark house.

The door groaned as I opened it slowly. I took a few steps into the laundry room and was greeted by my mother.

"Alexis!" she exclaimed as she nearly knocked me over trying to hug me. "You're okay!"

"Yeah, Mom, I'm okay," I said with relief. I was happy to be home, but I was also exhausted.

"What took you so long? Did you get lost?" Before I could answer, she examined my face closely and said, "Oh, thank goodness! You look so much better than you did in the car!"

"What do you mean I look so much better?" I asked suspiciously.

She pressed her lips tightly together and furrowed her eyebrows. Her eyes seemed to be somewhere else, somewhere she did not want to be. It took a moment before she spoke.

"Alexis, we need to talk. There are some things we need to figure out," she said.

My heart raced as my mind quickly ran through the countless things she might be worried about. I drew in a deep breath and nodded, then followed her into the living room.

We both sat down, but my mother looked tense. Her eyes were distant and preoccupied. She drew in a hollow breath before speaking.

"Alexis, I still can't read your mind. If there's something going on, you need to tell me," she said, utterly serious.

I looked at the floor as tears began trickling from my eyes. My mother put her arms around me and held me close. I laid my head in her lap and began to cry harder.

"Alexis, what is it? What are you not telling me?" she pleaded.

"So many things," I whimpered.

"Then tell me," she said as she stroked my hair. I sat up and took a deep breath before speaking.

"I've been having… dreams. Actually, they're more like nightmares," I said quietly and timidly.

"Okay, tell me what you've dreamed about."

I took a moment to gather my thoughts before I spoke. "It all started about two weeks ago. After I met Taylor, I dreamed that I was in the forest and I killed him. His face shattered before my eyes. Then, a strange man was standing between two trees and said, 'Look out because we're everywhere and everyone.' I couldn't see his face or anything—it was too dark—but it felt like I knew him. When he first saw me, he even said, 'It's been a long time,' like he knew who I was or something." I paused to let my mother think about what I had just said. After a minute, she finally spoke.

"What do you think the dream means?" she asked without meeting my eyes.

"I have no idea. I mean, it's just a dream, right?" I hoped she'd agree with me.

"It could be... but it could be more," she said, a hint of darkness in her voice.

"Well, if it really does mean something, then all I know is that there's a guy out there that I think I know, but don't know, who is out to get me." In the back of my mind, I couldn't help but think about my creepy encounter with that teacher on the day of the accident.

"Let's not go that far," Mom said, breaking my train of thought. "We don't know for sure what your dream means, but we will." Her voice had a note of false confidence.

I knew I had to tell her what had happened in the forest. If I wanted to figure out what my dream meant, then I had to let her know sooner or later.

"Mom, remember last week when I blacked out after running around in the forest?"

"Yeah," she answered

"Well, I lied when I said I didn't remember anything," I confessed.

"What… why didn't you tell me?" she asked, astonished.

"Because I had just found out about Andy, and I thought I was going insane. I saw things there that I didn't want to remember," I said, my voice filled with fear.

"What did you see?" she asked, intrigued.

"I… I saw the same exact trees from my dream in the forest." My mother pulled her eyebrows together and thought long and hard. After a moment, I caught her studying my face.

"What are you looking at?" I asked, feeling a bit self-conscious.

"I'm just trying to figure it out." She continued to stare at my face.

"Trying to figure out what?"

"Why your eyes have been changing colors," she said, as if I was supposed to know exactly what she was talking about.

"What? What do you mean?" I asked in confusion. "My eyes are the same color…." But my sentence trailed off as I realized what she meant.

"First, I saw that white ring around your eyes, and now this," she said, amazed.

"Now… what, Mom?"

"Don't worry, it's not as bad anymore," she said quickly, trying to ease my mind. It didn't work.

I jumped up from the couch and ran into my room, stopping in front of the wood-framed, full-length mirror. Then, I understood why my mother had been so terrified before I jumped out of the car.

The whites of my eyes were no longer white but stormy gray. Instead of the deep blue that usually surrounded my pupils, there was a dim green light.

I felt defeated. I had tried to be strong and good since I'd hurt Andy. My mind had been in turmoil, mostly because of what I'd done to him. Over the past couple of weeks, I'd had one weird nightmare after another and met a bizarre cast of characters. I'd been in the hospital after a panther attack. Now, my eyes were transforming before my… well, my eyes. I wanted to faint on the spot. I was already trembling and tearing up when I heard my mother come in and put her hands on my shoulders.

"Alexis, I know this is very stressful, but we need to figure out what's going on here. Do you understand?" she asked, quietly but firmly.

My only response was a weak nod. I heard my mother take a deep breath behind me before speaking.

"You said something about seeing the white ring before. When did you see it?" Her tone was so gentle that I turned and hugged her, finally ready to tell her everything.

ℭ𝔖

For the next twenty minutes, my mother and I sat on my bed and I told her about the two dreams that involved my eyes. I started with the first one, the one where Taylor tried to tell me something about Florida. After explaining every detail so that she didn't miss anything, I then told her about the dream with the coyote and the Native American girl who looked like me. She interrupted a few times to ask a question, but other than that, she remained calm and quiet. After I was finished, she sighed.

"Alexis, I'm really glad you told me all this," she began. "You have no idea how hard it is to understand you when I don't know what's going on in your head." She looked at me appreciatively as she spoke and held my weak hand in hers. I looked into her eyes and found that they were cloudy and distant.

"Mom, what's wrong?" I asked in an earnest tone. She blinked a few times and shook her head as she looked away from me. "Mom," I began, placing my free hand over hers. "I can tell something is going on with you, too. I'm sorry I've been too selfish to realize it before, but you have something to tell me. I can see it." Slowly, she turned her face back to mine. She pressed her lips together and closed her eyes.

"I don't want to scare you," she said, softly but darkly.

"Try me," I responded with false bravery. She paused and breathed out slowly.

"The black fog in your dream," she said quickly and quietly, as if the words burned her mouth.

"Yeah, what about it?" I asked, puzzled. She paused again and took another long breath before speaking.

"Every time I try to look inside your head, hear your thoughts, or control your emotions, all I see is a black fog. That's why I couldn't calm you down in the car," she explained.

I stared at her in astonishment. "But the panther, in the forest—you stopped me. If you hadn't, I would have killed him… right?"

She shook her head slowly and said, "Honey, you stopped yourself." Her voice held a hint of pride.

I was too amazed to speak, but my mind formed a million questions. Did I really stop myself from killing something? Was I finally learning to control myself? And how did all the strange dreams and experiences I'd been having relate to the changing color of my eyes? I thought I better ask the most important question before trying to figure out anything else.

"Why have I been seeing these things in my dreams?" I asked, a bit afraid of the answer I might get.

My mother squeezed my hand a little tighter and bit her bottom lip.

"Alexis, I don't think you're having dreams; I… I think you're having visions."

Chapter 10

When did life become so complicated? First, the unnatural strength; then, the speed; now all of a sudden, I was having visions? Just a month ago, I was a relatively normal teenager.

Sure, I was abnormally strong and fast, but I mostly managed to keep that a secret and fly under the radar. I hated school, but who didn't? I didn't have any friends, but that was for the best. Having friends meant sharing secrets, which meant danger. Obviously, I would rather have been completely normal, had friends, and had more fun at school, but since those things would never happen for me, I was generally able to put them out of my mind.

"*You can't seriously think that, can you?*"

"WILL YOU SHUT UP?!"I yelled out loud.

"What the... are you talking to me?" my mother asked impatiently.

"No, I wasn't talking to you, Mom." She gave me a weird look and continued to pack up our family pictures.

I know it seems like I was going crazy, but I swear I wasn't! It was just that, over the previous couple of weeks, the voice in my head had grown stronger. Every time I sat down to think, it talked back to me, and every time I was ready to take action, it told me to do something else. It seemed that the voice was trying to control me.

Okay, that explanation really didn't help my case for sanity.

"Alexis, what is with you?" Mom asked in a harsh tone.

"*Tell her. You promised her no more secrets. TELL HER,*" the voice urged.

I shook my head and answered, "Nothing. Sorry, I haven't had much sleep lately."

"*You're lying again. Why don't you just tell her?*"

"Why? Are you having dreams again?" Mom asked.

"*C'mon, Alexis… aren't you tired of lying?*"

"No, I'm just… nervous. That's all," I said as calmly as possible. Still, I was pretty sure she knew that I was lying.

"*Oh... you are SO lucky she can't read your mind! I have half a mind to tell her myself!*"

"*Yeah, right. How are you going to do that?*" I asked the voice.

I know, I know. The thing with the voice had gotten a little out of hand, but what was I going to tell my mother? "Mom, there's an annoying voice in my head talking to me and I'm talking back to it." Somehow, I didn't think that would make her less worried about me.

There was a short pause before my mom spoke.

"Alexis, are you lying to me?" she asked suspiciously.

I froze and felt my eyes grow wide.

"How do you like me now?" the voice mocked.

"*That was you? HOW?*" I thought to myself. I was freaking out. I wanted to know what was going on with the dreams—or visions or whatever—and, more important, how I could stop the voice inside my crazy head. But now wasn't the time to bring all that stuff up with my mother.

"I'm not lying to you, Mom. I'm just really nervous about going to a new school," I said. I could tell she didn't believe me, but there wasn't anything she could do about it, and she knew it.

"All right, just making sure," she said as she let out a breath of air. "You know what, why don't you go pack up your room? I think I've got this one under control."

"Are you sure? This is a big room."

"Yeah, I'm fine. Dr. Seymour is coming over to help in a little while anyway."

My body tensed up a bit and my voice became harder. "I still don't understand why he's going to move with us." My mother stopped what she was doing and shot me a harsh look of disbelief.

"Are we really going to go through that again?" she asked with a voice that matched her face.

"All I'm saying is that it seems like a lot for someone to just pick up and move to another state when he has a whole career and life going for him where he lives now, especially with his daughters. It's almost too much." I muttered that last part to myself, but my mother heard it.

Doc had two daughters who lived with him in Tennessee. Their mom had died giving birth to the younger one, Ella, who was now five years old. She was a cute kid… a little chatty but generally adorable. Doc's older daughter, Amy, was nine, but she was pretty mature for her age. In fact, she kind of reminded me of me. She was really cute, too. They were both lovable, and thankfully, Amy was a lot quieter than Ella.

"Doctor Seymour knows just as well as we do that it's going to be downright impossible to find a doctor for you that we can trust. Besides, he said he's ready for a change. Why is it so hard for you to accept him?" Mom asked in a more caring and tender voice.

"*Seriously, Alexis… why?*" the voice in my head asked even more gently.

"I... I don't know. It's just that, I see the way you guys act around each other, and I get defensive."

"Because of your father?" she asked carefully.

I didn't answer. I didn't want to answer. I wouldn't answer. I turned my back to her and said, "I have some packing to do." I could tell she wanted to push me to talk, but she knew better. She allowed me to go to my room without a fight.

ℭ

Before long, I had packed up almost everything in my room. All that was left was a mattress with two pillows and a small blanket on top of it, my backpack filled with some necessities, and a suitcase with about two weeks' worth of clothes.

I've only moved twice in my life, once when I about one or two and another time when I was about eight or nine. There was one other time when we thought we would have to move. That was back when I had the "incident" at Dr. Seymour's office. We were almost ready to flee to another state, when Dr. Seymour came to the door the following evening, swearing that he would never tell anyone our secret and promising that he would do all he could do to take care of us.

I know, I know.... He didn't seem like such a bad guy; in fact, he seemed like a great guy.

"*Then why do you have such a problem with him?*" the voice asked. This time, I didn't get mad. Come to think of it, I was remarkably calm.

"I wish I knew," I whispered to myself and the voice but heard no response. As I glanced around my now-empty room, I noticed something stacked up in the back of the closet.

I walked slowly across the cold, wooden floor to my white closet. I squatted down and picked up a big stack of textbooks and notebooks from school.

"Hey, Mom?" I shouted.

"Yes?" she answered.

"What do you want me to do with all my textbooks?" I asked as I ran my fingers lightly across the title of one the books in my hand.

"Make sure you don't have any of your papers in them, and we'll drop them off at the school when we leave."

I hauled the books over to my bed and began flipping through the pages. Every now and then, I'd come across a few papers. Some were notes and a lot of them were just doodles. After ten minutes, I had gone through each of my textbooks except for one, my Spanish book.

I slowly opened the front cover of the thin book, and immediately, a folded piece of paper dropped like a brick into my lap.

I knew instantly what it was, but I didn't know how to react. Time seemed to freeze. I stared at the note with my hands locked in place; there was no muscle movement in my body and no thoughts going through my mind. The note felt like a ten-pound weight on my lap, growing heavier and heavier by the second.

"*What are you waiting for?*" the voice asked. What *was* I waiting for? I was curious about what the note said, but something stopped me from picking it up and reading it.

I folded and refolded the note in half many times as I continued to debate with myself.

Or was I arguing with the voice in my head again? Ugh, I couldn't keep track! I might as well go crazy... at least then I would have a better excuse for hearing things.

I decided that I might as well read the note. Either I would drive myself fully insane by trying to guess what it might say or I would read it and feel terrible about myself. I think it was what they call a lose–lose situation. I slid my trembling finger between the two folded halves of the note and slowly opened the paper.

I briefly scanned the writing. The letters were just shy of illegible and written in blue ink. A lot of words were scratched out, but the note was about a full page long.

Before reading the letter, I closed my eyes, drew in a deep breath, and prayed that Andy hadn't written anything that would make me feel worse than I already did.

Alexis-

Hear me out. I-

Suddenly, I heard a light tap on my door that made me jump like a deer.

"Alexis?" a deep voice said. It was Dr. Seymour.

Irritated, I answered, "Yeah?"

"Your mother wants to know if you're all packed up for tomorrow," he said as he opened my bedroom door.

"Oh, I didn't know we were leaving tomorrow."

"Yeah, I found an apartment for myself and the girls near a hospital where I've been hired, and your mother found a house in the same area this morning. I thought she told you."

"Maybe she did. Anyway, yeah, I'm packed." I looked away from him and refocused on the note, now wrinkled from my tight hands.

"All right. The van's out front, so whenever you're ready, you can load up your junk," he said playfully.

I couldn't help but grin a little bit. Then I asked him, "Where are we moving to?"

"Florida," he said. As he walked away, I listened to his heavy shoes striking the hardwood floor; then, silence...

Chapter 11

You know that old saying "Everything happens for a reason"? I really hoped that whoever said that was wrong. I wasn't sure, but I thought that all the weird things I'd been experiencing were somehow connected. The dreams had to mean something. Even if they weren't visions, they obviously had some significance behind them.

Two or three weeks ago, I had dreamed about Taylor, and in that dream, he said something about being in Florida. Now, with a van full of our belongings behind us, we were about a half an hour outside of Jacksonville. That could not be a coincidence.

Dr. Seymour followed us in his car while my mother and I drove together in ours. A guy from the moving company brought up the rear with the van. My mom kept trying to start up conversation with me, but I kept my headphones clamped to my ears and stared out the window.

I didn't see many palm trees, which I thought was strange. The grass looked darker and rougher than the grass in Tennessee. I wasn't sure it would be comfortable to sit on.

As we neared Jacksonville, I began to feel queasy and nervous in the pit of my stomach, but at the same time, my heart raced with excitement. *Now what?* I wondered.

"*Maybe you're worried because you have to go to a new school tomorrow,*" the helpful voice in my head suggested.

But when I heard the voice, which was stronger than ever, I realized that I wasn't feeling nervous at all. I was excited and… happy.

"*You're back!*" I said to the voice, with a hint of enthusiasm.

"*Yes,*" the voice replied, "*but I won't be around for long.*"

"*Why?*" I asked, suddenly devastated. I felt stupid talking to the voice in my head, but I had grown to like it. It was kind of cool to have what felt like a whole separate person inside me, and the voice understood me… more than most people did anyway.

"*I'm sorry, Alexis, but I'll have to leave you soon. Maybe someday I'll be able to explain, but now is not the time.*" The voice sounded just as depressed as I did about saying goodbye. "*Besides, you won't need me for a while,*" it said in a lighter tone. "*Just remember that I'll be there for you in your time of greatest need.*"

I couldn't help but smile as I thought about the comforting and melodious voice, even though it was leaving me.

"*But you can't just leave. I need you.*" I felt pretty pathetic pleading to a fabrication of my thoughts, but I couldn't help myself.

The voice let out a quiet sigh, then said, "*Before long, my warrior.*"

"What are you so smiley about?" my mother asked with a light laugh.

Suddenly, my smile disappeared and my mind went blank.

଼

"Alexis, would you like to get room service?" my mother asked as I was getting ready for bed.

"No, thanks, I'm okay." I continued staring at myself in the mirror, just as I had been doing for ten or fifteen minutes. I wasn't even sure what I was looking at, or for, exactly.

I guess I was feeling a little alone without the voice.

I can't explain it, but I felt really connected to it. Now that it was gone, I didn't think it was a figment of my imagination. Maybe it was a conscience or some sort of guardian angel. All I knew was that I wished more than anything the voice was a real person that I could talk to.

"Are you sure you're all right?" Mom pressed. "You should eat."

Ordinarily, her questions would have completely aggravated me, but I was abnormally calm. I could feel her getting on my nerves, which would usually be cause for me to lose my temper, but I wasn't close to going even mildly berserk.

I finally broke my gaze from the mirror and walked out of the bathroom. I went to the side of one of the beds and sat down before answering.

"I'm not really hungry. Thanks, though," I said respectfully and quietly.

My mother studied my face for a moment and watched me as I rose and began to rummage around the hotel room for my backpack.

"Are you nervous?" she finally asked. I placed my backpack on the edge of the bed and began to fill it with supplies.

"Yeah," I answered quietly. My mother rose to give me a hug. Instead of pushing her away, I wrapped my arms tightly around her and cried softly. "I'm more than that," I sobbed. "I'm terrified." My mom held me tighter for a moment, then released her arms and took a step back.

"Alexis, listen to me." I raised my tear-filled eyes to hers as she began to speak. "This past month and a half has been difficult for both of us, but we can't let what happened in Tennessee hold us down forever." My vision had cleared up as my tears dried.

"But Andy… what if it happens again?" I asked, my throat sore and my voice shaky.

She took a deep, patient breath before answering. "Some people have trouble looking at the 'what ifs' in life. Others, like you, can't seem to stop thinking about them. Just remember what you know for certain, then you'll be able to handle the uncertainties later."

I wiped the remaining tears from my cheeks and nodded in

agreement. My mother put her arms around me one last time and said, "Whatever doesn't kill you makes you stronger."

I'd heard her say that before, and it seemed somewhat logical, but I always had a hard time truly believing it. I just nodded my head and pulled away.

"Go take a shower and get ready for bed," she said. "You have an early start tomorrow."

"What time do I have to get up?" I asked weakly.

"Six o'clock."

Oh, this was going to be fun… I could tell already.

ɷ

The passing scenery was dreary and dark as we drove. My mother, her face filled with both excitement and worry, could not stop talking. I, on the other hand, would have given anything for another ten minutes in bed. I stared out the window, my heart pounding and my palms sweaty with anxiety. My nervous hands played with my khaki skirt while thousands of questions buzzed around in my head like a swarm of angry bees.

What if it happens again? Am I strong enough to control myself, like I did in the forest? Is there a reason I'm in Florida? Does someone need me here? Is that why I dreamed about coming here? Is it Taylor who needs me? I laughed a little at that last one. Obviously, I would never see him again; I might as well get over it.

My heart sank when I thought about not seeing Taylor again. It was true, and I knew it.

"Here we are," my mother said in a squeaky voice. She sounded like a hamster on steroids.

I looked out the window at my new high school, Jacksonville Christian School. It was small, but private schools are usually small. The walls were made of red bricks and the doors were dark wood. It looked cozy; I'll give it that. But I doubted that I was going to like it there.

A small number of older-looking high school kids were pulling their cars into their assigned spots; some were already walking up the sidewalk and into the open hallway. A number of them stared at us as they walked by, which didn't make me feel too welcome.

"Have a great day, Alexis," my mom said sincerely. She wrapped one arm around me and kissed me on the cheek. Thank goodness no one saw.

"Thanks," I mumbled as I climbed slowly out of the car. I walked up to the sidewalk and turned around to see my mother drive quickly away, but not quick enough that I couldn't see the tears running down her face.

☙

I walked through a door that said "High School Building" and followed the signs to the office. I cleared my throat nervously and spoke to the woman sitting at the front desk. "Hi, uh... I'm Alexis.

This is my first day." I spoke so quietly that I was surprised she could hear me.

She looked up from her paperwork and smiled at me. She had beautiful tan skin and shoulder-length hair that was perfectly styled. She didn't look any older than my mother, maybe even younger.

"Hi, Alexis," she said with a light southern accent and a beautiful white smile. "I'm Mrs. Kinder. Welcome to JCS. Let's get you started." She got up from her chair and began digging through a filing cabinet behind her. "What's your last name?"

"Randall, Alexis Randall," I informed her.

"Randall… Randall…," she mumbled to herself as she searched. "Ah, here we are," she said, closing the cabinet and placing a folder on her desk.

I walked up closer to the desk to see what she had for me.

"Okay, in here is your schedule, a lunch order form, an order form for spirit day clothes, and some paperwork for your mom," she said as she thumbed through the folder.

"What's spirit day?" I asked.

"On the first Friday of every month, you get to wear jeans and a spirit day shirt or any school shirt," she explained.

"Okay." That was pretty cool, I had to admit. I didn't know private schools did things like that.

Mrs. Kinder continued: "You know that today's a half day, right?"

"Yes, ma'am. My mom knows to pick me up at eleven."

"Perfect. Remember that we have half days on the first Wednesday of every month," she informed me.

Maybe I had been wrong about this place. It didn't seem as horrible as I thought it would be. But the day was young; something dreadful could still happen.

I took out my schedule and read over it. I studied my classes for a minute before Mrs. Kinder handed me a small map of the school and a tiny slip of paper.

"That paper has your locker number and combination," she explained.

"Okay."

"You have all of your books, correct?" she asked.

"Yes, ma'am," I answered shyly.

"Okay, then you're good to go. If you need anything at all, just come and see me," she said with a sincere smile.

"Thank you," I said again as I turned and walked out of the office and into the open hallway, which was now filled with students.

☙

I tried to ignore the fact that everyone was staring at me. I tried to ignore the whispers I heard behind me. I also tried to control my anger level. But I seemed to be failing at all three attempts. As I placed each textbook into my locker, I tried to think of places I could run if the power became too much to bear. As I considered my options, a voice from behind me literally made me jump.

"Hey!"

After my heart dropped back down to normal speed, I squeezed my eyes shut, took a deep calming breath, and turned around.

My eyes met those of a tall, redheaded girl. She had soft hazel eyes, light freckles across her nose, and a pretty smile. She seemed like one of those goody-goody girls who was always the first to sit by a lonely loser at a lunch table. Given that she was talking to me, my assessment was probably right.

"Hi," I responded, agitated.

"I'm Christy," she said.

"Alexis," I replied as I grabbed my gym bag and shut my locker door. When I turned back around, she noticed what I was holding.

"Oh, you're in P.E. first period?" she asked kindly.

"Yeah," I answered shortly. There was a slight pause before she asked another question. "Do you know where everything is?"

I couldn't tell what her deal was. Did I look like that much of a loser that she felt she needed to babysit me, or did she not have any other friends and desperately wanted me to be her freaking BFF? Either way, I wanted her to go away.

"Thanks, Christy, but I'm perfectly capable of figuring out how to get to the gym for myself." I felt kind of bad about being so rude, but it seemed like the only way to get rid of her.

"Okay, then," she answered, sounding hurt. "If you need anything, I'd be happy to help you." She turned her back to me and started to walk away.

Oh no, I thought to myself. I'd only been at school for twenty minutes, and already, I was attached to someone.

"Christy, wai– ," I started, but before I could go after her, I heard someone behind me.

"Alexis!?" a strong, firm voice exclaimed in a surprised tone.

I turned around and was completely and utterly shocked at who I saw. My body froze and my mind went totally blank.

Those dark eyes… the perfect, gleaming smile...

I couldn't believe it; he was actually here.

Chapter 12

I didn't know what to think. I didn't know how to react. I didn't even know how to feel!

Shocked? Yes. Terrified? Possibly. Ecstatic? Not too sure; I'll chew on that one later. Confused? More than a kindergartner in trigonometry.

All I *could* do was stare, my eyes threatening to pop out of their sockets and zoom back in as if I was a cartoon character.

"Wow!" he exclaimed. "I– I–… I can't believe it! What are the odds? I mean… WOW!" he repeated.

I remained standing by my locker, dumbfounded. After a short pause, I managed to emit an "uhh."

His expression relaxed a bit, but he still had puppy-like excitement written on his face. "What are you doing here? Did you move away from Tennessee?" he asked quickly.

Part of me wanted to blurt out, "Oh, so NOW you care?" But I didn't want to drive him away immediately, so I responded as best I could.

"Um, yeah, we moved… here," I answered in a small, weak voice. He continued to stare at me in amazement.

The real question was: What was *he* doing here? The last time I saw him was in Tennessee. But now he was in Florida, too? Had my dream really been a vision of the future? Was he stalking me? Did he think *I* was stalking *him*?! I couldn't deal with all these questions at once. Stray thoughts, images from dreams, and echoes of voices began spiraling and spinning in my mind.

"This is just amazing!" he exclaimed, again with disbelief.

I was starting to get lightheaded from everything that was swirling through my head. I managed to nod as I stared at his feet.

His face melted into concern, and he said, "Are you okay, Alexis?"

I couldn't mutter a single clear word. I tried saying, "I'm just shocked," but it came out more like "juts shucked."

I'm sure I sounded breathtakingly intelligent.

He stared at me with a blank expression and empty eyes, not understanding a word I had said. I felt my face grow red hot with humiliation.

He opened his mouth to speak, but I beat him to the punch (not literally, thank God). "I've got to go," I said and spun on my heels to walk quickly away. (I mean, a Normal definition of quick, not *my* definition, of course.)

I heard him call out to me, but I ignored him. I felt a tug at my gut and a sinking feeling in my heart. Something was stirring inside me. It felt like the first battle in a war between my logic, my instincts, and my emotions.

Logically, I knew I couldn't associate with Normals, which meant *all* Normals. NO EXCEPTIONS. Emotionally, however, I *really* wanted to make an exception for Taylor. No matter how much my logic tried to deny it, I knew we were attracted to each other, which might actually be good for me. My instincts don't usually show up unless the issue is important. They act like a magnet, if that makes any sense, pulling or pushing me in the right direction. Basically, my gut was telling me to go back and talk to Taylor. But I let logic win this round, and I continued to the gym.

Another part of me desperately wanted to at least turn around and look at him, as if it was the last time I might seem him before he disappeared.

Hey, my thoughts weren't totally crazy, right? I'd already had a dream where his face shattered before my eyes.

I had reached the end of the hall where the gym was and opened the glass door. I took one step in before I involuntarily turned around to see Taylor.

I couldn't see his face well from my position, but I could tell his expression was one of hurt. I felt my heart swell with the overwhelming urge to run to him. For a split second, I thought about doing just that. Then, I felt an icy hand on my shoulder that made my heart skip a beat and my entire body flush with adrenalin.

"Oops, I'm sorry! Did I scare you?" an upbeat but nasally voice said.

I spun around with anger and met a pair of gray eyes.

"No, my heart just needs restarting, that's all," I said furiously.

The girl I was talking to had black hair and pale skin. She was wearing a JCS soccer sweatshirt. I found the sports sweatshirt surprising. I didn't mean to be judgmental or anything, but she didn't seem like a jock.

"Sorry," she fired back defensively. "I didn't mean to startle you."

"Maybe you should work on that. Start with not sneaking up on people," I said with all the sarcasm I could muster.

"Excuse me?" she said in the same tone that a mother uses when her kid smarts off.

"You heard me."

"Honey, if you want to get along in this school, I suggest you start recognizing who's important," the girl said, a hint of both snobby and sassy in her voice.

Who did this girl think she was? I was so ready to smack her across the face. Of course, if she kept up her attitude, she would get something even worse.

"Let me guess, Miss High School, I should be nice to you?" I asked edgily.

"That's right, sweetheart; don't mess with me. I have more connections here than you will ever have in your entire life. I have the power to make your life here a living hell." Her tone was threatening, but I was hardly scared. If I could kick a panther's butt with my bare hands, I could deal with her.

I'd had about enough of this chick. I took a step forward and got right in her face (at least as much in her face as a five foot person could get). "Oh, I'm terrified," I said in a deadly tone.

She let out a huff of breath and stormed out of the gym.

I could tell that this encounter with Miss High School would be the first of many to come.

I rolled my eyes and shook it off. When I turned around, I saw two tall girls approaching me. One of them was laughing, but the other's expression was hard to read.

"Oh wow, nicely done!" the taller of the two exclaimed. She had vibrant blue eyes and long, curly, blonde hair.

"I have to say, that may be the highlight of my week!" the other blonde girl added. She also had the soccer sweatshirt on, and she seemed more like a sporty type.

She had long, straight hair and pretty green eyes.

"Glad I could provide you with some entertainment," I said.

"Yeah, that was great. Anyway, I'm Ariella," the green-eyed blonde said, still laughing.

"And I'm Sophia," the taller blonde said, trying to smother her giggles.

"Alexis," I quickly introduced myself. "Is that girl always so…" Before I could finish my question, they had the answer.

"Oh yeah," Ariella said, again bursting into laughter. Sophia elbowed her in the side and gave her a disapproving look, but Ariella continued to chuckle.

"Mandy has her moments, but when you get to know her, she can be all right," Sophia explained. For a second, I felt like laughing as hard as Ariella was.

I let out a small giggle before I snapped back to reality. Once again, I was talking and associating with Normals, breaking rule numero uno on the first day of school. Logic took over, and my expression turned hard and serious.

"Nice to meet you," I muttered as I power-walked past Ariella and Sophia.

Ugh. Note to self: I'd have to be careful here. My goal was to blend in, not call attention to myself.

ଓଃ

My morning hadn't gone too smoothly. Actually, I marked it down as a DISASTER. First, Taylor was here; that problem was self-explanatory. Second, I almost got into it with Mandy, aka my new enemy. Finally, for the icing on the cake, I broke the most important rule of my life.

On the plus side, I…. Oh, that's right; there wasn't a plus side.

I guess P.E. didn't go as horrifically as I thought it would. I didn't have the JCS gym clothes, so the coach let me sit out. For second period, the same coach taught personal fitness, which wasn't too bad either. He talked a lot while the other students and I took notes or spaced out. As I walked into third period, though, I knew my day was about to go downhill.

"Ah, yes. Alexis Randall. Welcome to Algebra I!" Mrs. Tanner said excitedly.

Ugh, math. The very thought of it makes my stomach churn.

"I'll fill you in on where we are in the textbook later. In the meantime, go ahead and take a seat right over…." Her voice trailed off as she scanned the room for an empty desk. "Ah, right behind Mr. Mason over there." She pointed toward one of the seats in the back of the class. One boy popped his head up and smiled when he saw me. I assumed he was "Mr. Mason."

I walked to a seat that was up against the back wall and sat down. Mrs. Tanner began the lesson as I settled in and got organized. A few minutes into the class, the kid in front of me turned in his chair to look at me.

"Wow, only five minutes and already I'm bored outta my mind," he said. I couldn't help but grin a little bit.

"Yeah, tell me about it," I answered, trying to keep my smile under control.

"Hey, I'm Evan," he said. Mrs. Tanner shushed him to be quiet, so he turned back around to face the board.

I leaned over my desk a little bit and whispered, "I'm Alexis."

He turned his head very slightly to the right and whispered back, "Nice to meet you."

I focused my eyes back on the white board as my mind began to drift. Once again, it took me a few minutes to realize what I had just done.

DAMN IT! I thought.

What was wrong with me today? Was I TRYING to destroy myself? Gosh, I can be such an idiot!

"*Have you ever thought that maybe it's not such a bad idea to let new people into your life?*" the voice said.

My heart skipped excitedly when I heard it, and I felt my lips twitch into a smile. My old friend sounded faint and distant, but I understood clearly what it had said … if that makes any sense.

I was so delighted to hear the voice again that I didn't realize Mrs.

Tanner was standing by my desk until she cleared her throat to get my attention.

"Did you happen to catch a word I said up there, Ms. Randall?" she asked, half-mockingly.

"Uh, not really," I answered.

She sighed heavily but said, "Since it's your first day and I'm in a generous mood, I'll let you try the homework for tonight and I won't count it for a grade. But I do suggest that you pay attention in class." She walked away from my desk and left me feeling embarrassed.

I guess I could probably mark her down as enemy number two. Dang, I was on a roll.

Evan turned back around to me after Mrs. Tanner had walked away and said, "You should see her when she's in a *bad* mood."

Once again, I couldn't stop myself from laughing. "I bet that's fun," I replied. Evan laughed, too, and Mrs. T shushed us again, which of course, made it all the more difficult to stop laughing.

The logical part of my mind pushed its way to the front once again. I hardened my expression and pretended to be busy with my notes, hoping that Evan would get the hint and leave me alone.

A moment passed before he spoke again. "What school did you go to before you came here?" he asked casually.

I immediately froze. I didn't want to answer, but I couldn't just sit there and stare at this kid like an idiot! I was about to say something when Mrs. T interrupted.

"All right, class, have a good rest of the day," she said dryly.

PHEW! Talk about saved by the bell!

I quickly grabbed my things and darted out the door before anyone else could talk to me.

☙

The rest of the day went by pretty quickly, partially because we got out of school at eleven o'clock. The rest of my classes were almost as difficult as math, but I didn't mind. If we all had to concentrate, it meant that there were fewer opportunities for people to talk to me.

Once my Bible class was out, I went to my locker to collect my stuff. I was glad that I had only a few things to do for homework. While I was packing up my book bag, I heard a familiar, perky voice from behind me.

"So? How was it?" Christy asked excitedly. I stood up and closed my locker door before I responded.

"How was what?" I asked, confused.

"Your first day, silly!" she exclaimed. "How was it?"

"Okay, I guess," I answered uncomfortably.

There was a long, awkward silence before she spoke again.

"Listen, I'm sorry if I got on your nerves this morning. I was just trying to make sure you were okay." Her voice sounded weak.

Oh crap.

"No, I'm sorry I snapped," I said sincerely. "I just had a lot on my mind. No hard feelings?" I asked.

Christy's face brightened when I finished. "Of course not!" she said. "No problem!"

"Okay," I replied awkwardly.

"Would you like to sit with me and my friends tomorrow?" she asked ecstatically.

I thought for a moment, and I STILL can't believe I said this.... "Sure, why not?" (although I probably could have cited about a hundred and fifty reasons why not). I couldn't help but give in to her... she was just trying to be nice.

"Awesome! See you tomorrow!" Christy said as she wrapped her arms around me and gave me a quick hug.

My body tensed and my hands clenched as I froze into position. She immediately let go and pranced off in the other direction.

Wow, that was one happy kid.

I slowly shook off the surprise hug attack and picked up my backpack. I turned around and immediately saw Taylor at the end of the long hall.

His eyes were dark and unreadable as he gazed at me. He was leaning up against a locker, and his muscular arms were crossed in front of his chest. After a moment of eye contact, he grinned. His perfect white teeth barely peeked through his flawless lips, making him look absolutely amazing, like a male model.

I wanted to smile back, run to him, or at least talk to him. But then, I came back to my senses. All of a sudden, I was overwhelmed by countless emotions: pain, happiness, anger, anxiety, bliss, sadness, and most of all, confusion.

Oh, the joys of being a teenager.

I tore my gaze from his and walked out to the car line so I could get out of this place before anything worse happened.

Checking my phone, I saw that I'd gotten a text from my darling mother, saying that she would be about fifteen minutes late. Standing outside wouldn't have been a big deal, except that my new "friend" Mandy and I were the only ones still waiting for our parents to pick us up.

AWKWARD....

I stood at one end of the sidewalk and she kept to the other. We stayed like that for about five minutes, until she approached me.

"Hey, listen, this morning was... well, not very pleasant. I didn't mean to make your first day difficult. I just don't want you to have a problem with me. Are we okay?"

Wow, that was probably the weakest apology ever. But hey, it was something.

"Yeah, I guess," I answered. She nodded her head and kept her eyes away from mine.

"By the way, I'm Mandy," she said. I took a patient breath and responded.

"Alexis." We stood next to each other in uncomfortable silence for what felt like hours until my mom *finally* pulled up.

"All right, well, that's my ride," I said uneasily as I began to walk away.

"Okay, see you tomorrow!" she called as I got into the car.

My mom pulled out of the school parking lot as I settled into my seat and threw my backpack into the back of the car.

"So? How was school?" Mom asked excitedly.

Hah, should I start with the bad part or the REALLY bad part?

Chapter 13

"I had a dream that Taylor and I were in Florida. And, unless I have COMPLETELY lost my sanity, Taylor goes to my school, which happens to be in Florida," I reminded my mother as I sat at the desk in the hotel room, looking up some information on the Internet.

She took in a deep, thoughtful breath as she paced the length of our room. "Let me get this straight," she finally said. "In these past couple months, you have had two significant dreams, the dream with the mysterious man and the trees, and the eye color, fog, and Florida dream. Almost everything in both dreams has come true."

Thank you, Mother, for the daily dose of DUH!

"Yeah, so?" I asked, a bit impatiently.

"I'm trying to decide if these are real visions or…." She let her sentence trail off.

"Or… what, Mom?" I asked, suddenly anxious. She lifted her gaze from the green carpet and looked at me.

"Nothing, maybe they're just nothing," she said absently.

"Mom, usually I would agree with that, but I think these things are connected somehow. Everything that has been happening to me has a reason behind it," I said.

My mom looked away and began pacing, thinking again. I closed the laptop and leaned back in the thick leather swivel chair, rubbing my temples to somehow massage my problems away.

"This is very interesting," my mother said as she pondered her own thoughts. I stared at her in disbelief.

"Interesting? That's the appropriate word to describe this whole thing? INTERESTING?" I asked angrily.

I stood up, almost knocking the desk over, and faced my mother with wild eyes.

"Whoa, it's okay, Alexis. I didn't mean anything," she replied. She tried to keep her voice level, but I could see that she was alarmed.

I felt my veins grow hot and my mind become agitated. I took a few forceful steps toward her, and she flinched.

For a moment, I felt like crying. My own mother was afraid I was going to hurt her, and the sad thing was, it was always a possibility.

"I'm going running," I said tensely as I stormed past Mom. My hand reached for the door, but she caught me by my shoulder.

"No, absolutely not. You do not know the area well enough yet. Besides, it's good practice to try to control yourself." She sounded brave, but bravery wouldn't protect her once my curse took over.

"My other alternative?" I said through my clenched jaw. My anger was growing; I could already feel my arms and legs starting to go numb.

"Stay here and restrain yourself. You've done it before, and I bet with practice, we can crack the code," she said solemnly. I slowly turned around and faced her. Her eyes grew large and she began to cower.

"Crack what code exactly?" I asked with death in my voice and rage in my eyes. "Do you think there's some secret to my curse? Well, sorry to spoil your surprise, but there is no secret. No trick, no code, no strings attached. The truth is that I'm a monster. Have you ever heard of the boogey man trying to make friends and pretend to be a normal person? HUH?!" I shouted.

She started to back away, but I advanced toward her.

"I will never be close with a Normal, nor will I ever want to be. Do you know why?" I taunted. "Because I AM NOT NORMAL. Do you hear me? NOT THE LEAST BIT! Do you know what happens when I TRY to be Normal? I'll tell you what happens." My voice became deadly flat and quiet as I answered my own question: "People get hurt, Mother." I paused for a moment before continuing. "Are you saying that we should use YOU as a guinea pig, to see if I don't attack you? Because it's starting to seem that way."

She continued to stare, and I did the same. Her face had become more terrified with every word I said.

I had backed my mom up against a wall. No way could she run; she had no chance of fighting back; and jumping out the window of a ten-story hotel wasn't a good idea. Without my mom's powers, she was going to die.

My arms tightened and my body began to sink to the floor: the attack position.

My mind raced with images and thoughts. If the inside of my brain were a movie, it would cause epileptic seizures. My inner self was torn in half. One second, I was set on attacking my own mother (my curse talking), and the next second, I was able to think clearly.

Still, the curse was winning. I was in a full crouch position, ready to strike, when something happened.

My body locked up and my thoughts came to a screeching halt. There was a moment of darkness; then I heard a crash.

ꕤ

As I drifted in the dark, all I could think was, *Oh no, oh no, oh no. I hurt Mom. Oh God, did I kill her?*

I could not contemplate my life without her or with the knowledge that I had harmed her in any way.

I struggled to bring myself to consciousness. My whole body ached and my eyes were sore, as if I had been crying again. My mind was fuzzy, but it was no longer a train wreck of disconnected thoughts.

I couldn't tell if I had gone into a coma again or passed out. I knew I wasn't dead because I could feel pain. Unless I was on my way to hell.... I wouldn't be surprised if I was.

"Alexis, Alexis.... Can you hear me?" I heard a familiar masculine voice ask.

It was Dr. Seymour, but I also heard someone else.

"Alexis, honey? Please wake up!" The voice seemed desperate.

It sounded like... but it couldn't be...

Finally, my eyes opened. The lights in the room momentarily blinded me, but I quickly regained my sight.

I looked around to see who I had heard. Dr Seymour was standing over me with someone by his side.

She had been crying, but when she met my gaze, her face lit up with relief and joy.

"ALEXIS!" she exclaimed as she propped me upright on the bed and gave me a huge hug. "Honey, I– I– I can't, I mean...." She took a moment to collect herself. "What happened?" she asked anxiously.

I stared at her, horrified.

"Alexis, what's wrong?" she asked.

"I thought you... died." She frowned and looked perplexed. "I thought I killed you. Is this a dream? Oh my God, AM I DEAD?" I started hyperventilating, and terror rushed into my brain. I felt as if someone had finally cracked the fragile egg that contained my sanity. My eyes went wide with fear and my body trembled. I searched the room frantically for an exit and, for a second, seriously considered the window.

"Alexis, calm down. You're not dead and neither is your mother," Dr. Seymour said in a remarkably calm tone.

Believe it or not, I actually chilled out. Wow, this guy was good.

"But how?" I asked as I looked at my mother. She shook her head and shrugged her shoulders with uncertainty.

"To tell you the truth, I thought I was done for, too, but you just… passed out," she said.

"Are you sure you didn't do something? I kind of feel like I've been mind-wiped."

"Positive. I tried to control you, but I still couldn't get past the black fog."

We were all at a loss. I thought I could break the tension by saying something to make my mom feel better.

"Mom, maybe I… did that to myself." Her eyes widened and her mouth dropped open a little bit. Dr. Seymour studied my face with curiosity, probably wondering if I had suffered brain damage. "Think about it, Mom; if you didn't do it, what other possibility is there?" I asked logically.

She seemed to consider my question, while Dr. Seymour continued to examine my face. Finally, my mother answered.

"You may be right, but let's not jump to conclusions. The important thing is that you and I are both safe." She reached over and hugged me again, more gently this time.

When she released me, I looked over at Dr. Seymour. He was STILL staring at me.

Noticing his behavior, my mom asked, "Um, is there something wrong, Kent?"

"Her... her...," he faltered.

Mom was bewildered. "What are you talking about?"

Take a wild guess.

"He's talking about my eyes, Mom." I pointed to my gray corneas and the fading green light in them.

"Ah... that's right. We forgot to tell you about that," my mother said casually.

"You mean this has happened before?" he asked, astonished.

"Yeah," I said.

"A couple of times..." my mother replied.

Dr. Seymour's eyes bounced back and forth between us, as if he was watching a particularly exciting ping-pong match.

"Let's think about what we know and what we don't know," Mom said, ignoring the doctor's distress.

"We know you couldn't stop my powers, but we don't know for sure if I stopped myself."

"We know that your dreams have been coming true, but don't know if they're visions or not," my mother added.

"And we know your eyes change colors, but do we know why?" Dr. Seymour asked.

My mother and I exchanged a puzzled look.

We had never even addressed that issue. Now that I thought about it, it might be interesting to find out why that was happening.

"I didn't even think about that," my mother said in a low voice. Her eyes were still wide, but now her eyebrows were slightly pulled together: a sure sign that she was deep in thought.

I shifted my gaze from Mom to Dr. S. He was staring at her with a thoughtful and concerned expression.

I couldn't deny it. There was definitely something between them, whether or not they admitted it. Sensing their chemistry made me upset, which in turn, made me feel guilty. But still, their mutual attraction got under my skin. I mean, come on.... She's my *mom*. I want to look after her.

I remembered an incident from back when I was in kindergarten. I was on the playground and everything was hunky-dory until a snot-nosed punk stole my ball and started making fun of me. (At the time, I wasn't fully aware of the extent of my powers.) I got upset and started crying. Then, the kid made the biggest mistake of his life. He said, "Did your mommy cry that bad when your daddy left?" That was the day I found out I could launch a kid about a hundred feet across a playground and knock down a jungle gym.

Childhood was peachy from then on.

After a visit to the principal's office and a conference in which my mother did some pretty fast talking, she said to me, "Alexis, no matter what someone says to you or what kind of bad situation you find yourself in, it's not your job to protect me. It's MY job to protect YOU."

Even now that I'm a teenager, she still gives me the same speech sometimes. But regardless of how many lectures she gives me, I always will shield her. Even though she says it's not my duty, it sort of is. I can't help it. Defending her is in my blood; it's my instinct.

"*Following logic can sometimes lead to logical disaster; following emotions is a precarious path, but instinct is God's way of leading us to our destiny.*" The voice was still faint, but the words pierced right through me.

Chapter 14

The clear, sunny skies faded behind me as I continued down the long, empty hallway. The tile floor was littered with papers and the occasional flattened piece of gum. The school had an eerie stillness to it as I dragged myself to my locker.

I had slept in this morning and was late, so I was alone. It was just me, the forgotten lockers, and the abandoned hall.

As I was putting my books away, I heard faint footsteps coming from around the corner. I kept my eyes in my locker and began sorting faster through my notebooks, trying to find my homework.

"Ugh, this is the LAST place I want to be," a young voice said.

I looked behind me and saw a tall, skinny girl with light brunette hair. Her back was to me at first, but once she had her locker opened, she glanced at me with fierce green eyes. I don't mean green like bright green eyes. I mean *fierce* green, as if they were two glowing gems. They almost seemed unreal.

I shuddered at the intensity of her stare before responding.

"Yeah, tell me about it."

"I'm May. What grade are you in?" she asked casually as she turned her back to me once again to put her books away.

"Alexis," I said closing my locker, "and I'm a sophomore." I stood up and was ready to walk away, but she stopped me before I had the chance.

"Cool, I'm a freshman."

Like I cared; I just wanted to get out of there.

"Listen, come sit with me at lunch." That didn't sound so much like an offer as an order. She still hadn't looked directly at me, which I found strange.

"Um, that's okay. Thanks though," I said awkwardly. There was a small pause, so I began to walk away.

"Why not?" she asked. She sounded as if she was hurt but trying not to show it.

"Oh, it's just that Christy asked me to sit with her today, and she's kind of been helping me out," I said unsteadily.

There was another short, apprehensive silence before she closed her locker door and turned to look at me.

Her gaze took my breath away. Her eyes seemed even more ferocious, as if they were reflecting fire. Her look was steady but not unwelcoming. I couldn't have looked away even if I wanted to.

"I wouldn't sit with her. She's just being nice to you because you're the poor new girl who needs a friend. She's not really your friend; she just feels bad for you. She pities you."

My mind went blank for a second, but then the truth of May's statement hit me. She had a point. It did seem like Christy was more interested in checking out the new girl than getting to know the real me. Of course, I didn't care either way because I didn't want to make friends with Normals, but still, a little sincerity would be nice!

"Come sit with me… that's a real invite," May said.

I don't know what came over me, but I actually said, "Yes, thanks May."

She grinned and said, "No problem."

Suddenly, classroom doors on either side of the hall opened, and swarms of students streamed out. May glanced away from me for a second. Now that we were no longer alone, she looked almost… disgusted?

"See you at lunch, Alexis," she grumbled as she walked swiftly down the busy hallway.

I stood still for a moment, wondering what had impelled me to accept May's invitation. After a second or two, my brain checked back in and I headed off to my next class.

ଓ

Fifth-period English was almost over, and I was extremely nervous.

Somehow, agreeing to have lunch with May felt like a mistake, a bad one.

"All right, class, you're excused," Mrs. Hill said as she walked to her desk and began to organize her papers.

Maybe May forgot all about inviting me to sit with her. It was possible, right?

I gathered my things and made my way to the door. I was the last one out of the classroom and was praying that May had forgotten about me or simply wouldn't see me.

Of course, my life had never been that easy.

Before I could even take two steps out the classroom door, she was there, standing only a few feet away and looking at me with her severe eyes and soft face. I couldn't really describe her expression. Written on her face was a look of innocence, but she gave off a vibe that said, "Screw with me and you will soon be praying for mercy."

Hey, at least we had some common ground!

"Hey, Alexis!" she exclaimed with sudden eagerness. Her eyes melted from intense concentration to a chipper and flighty joy.

"Hi, May," I said with weak excitement.

Her bounciness seemed at odds with the earlier impression I had gotten of her. Maybe she had some kind of a split personality.

Better watch out for this one…

ଓ

"... and then, no joke, she came out soaking wet, covered head to toe with God knows what!" May exclaimed.

We both broke into hysterical laughter. I leaned back so far that I almost flipped off the bench.

Nope, you're not dreaming. I, Alexis Randall, was actually talking and hanging out with a *Normal*! (Dramatic gasps.) I know, I know... I've ranted about how dangerous it is for me to be around Normals, and trust me, that rule hadn't changed. I was still on my guard and still got twitchy when I was too close to them in a small space.

But this felt different. May didn't seem like other Normals—not feeble or defenseless. I was betting that she could hold her own against almost anything... but that didn't mean my rule had changed.

"Oh, oh, oh my gosh!" I said, gasping for breath and trembling with giggles.

"I knowwww!" she replied, trying to calm herself.

After another moment of trying to smother our laughter, May finally drew in enough breath to speak.

"Ahh, yeah, so... where did you move from again?" she asked, almost panting.

"Chattanooga, in Tennessee," I responded, still a bit lightheaded.

"Oh, very cool!" she said, "I have a friend up there who rides horses. Do you ride?" she asked casually.

"No, well… when I was younger, yeah, but I stopped a few years ago."

"What made you give it up?" she asked, stunned. "If I had a horse, I don't think I'd ever part from it."

It was true; I used to ride horses as a kid, and I had been pretty good. When I thought about it, I could still feel the warm sun on my back and the wind gently tossing my hair as I rode. My horse and I shared a bond; he responded to my commands without question, but I sensed that he felt the joy and freedom of the experience as much as I did. The two of us had loved and trusted each other. By the time I moved to Florida, though, all that was in the past.

"My horse died in a freak accident," I answered, my voice quiet and rough. The thought of that day still saddened me.

"Oh my God, I'm so sorry!" May said sincerely.

"It's cool now," I lied.

Suddenly, I felt someone behind me, tapping my shoulder. Before I turned, I took a quick glance at May. She looked up and was smiling. Her eyes grew soft and sweet and her head tilted slightly to the side.

When I looked cautiously behind me, I met Taylor's stunning eyes.

"Hey," he said with no smile. His expression was hard to read, but his eyes seemed troubled as he looked down at me.

"Hi, Taylor," May said with adoration. I immediately shot her a look.

Since when did she become so warm and friendly? And what was with the puppy eyes? I tried not to scowl at her, but I couldn't help it.

"Oh, hey, May," Taylor said, as if he had just noticed her presence. "Listen, can we talk?"

"Of course, we can! Alexis, do you mind?" May turned to me, widening her eyes. I gathered my lunch things and was ready to haul you-know-what out of there when…

"Oh, sorry, May, but I was talking to Alexis," Taylor said. I practically choked on my drink.

May looked at Taylor with flushed cheeks, then turned to me and glowered. She picked up her stuff and muttered something as she walked away.

Taylor walked around the table to the bench that was directly across from me.

What in the world did he want from me? Was he trying to make my life complicated? Ugh, I just couldn't catch a break.

"So," he began, "why do I get the feeling that you've been avoiding me?"

I took a moment to gather my thoughts, so I wouldn't blow up with words and fury.

"I don't know. There's just… a lot." Wow, great explanation, Alexis! That made *perfect* sense!

He chuckled for a moment and continued, "Like?"

"I don't know. It's just weird." At least that seemed like some progress.

"Why? Because I was in Tennessee and now I'm here?" he asked.

His guess was actually exactly right. Was he thinking the same thing I was?

"Yeah, why are you here?" I asked, a bit hostile.

"I was visiting some family up in Chattanooga, but I live here with Mark," he answered simply.

"Oh, cool." Why did this whole conversation feel so awkward? There was no reason for me to be so uncomfortable around him, but I was. "But I thought you were homeschooled?"

He paused for a moment before saying, "Oh, Mark finally gave in and let me go to a regular school. I just started going here a few weeks ago."

I nodded as my eyes dropped to the ground.

"You still haven't answered my question: Why are you avoiding me?"

Why was he even bothering with me?

"I don't know," I responded, yet again.

Actually, the truth was that I did know. Even though I liked him, the fact of the matter was that it was too dangerous for him to be around me—let alone for us to have a relationship.

If he even wanted to, which I was still not sure of.

The only way to keep him safe was to stay away from him, even if it hurt.

"You know what I think," he said softly, leaning slightly across the table. "I think you sense the chemistry between us, and that intimidates you."

I looked away with humiliation. I felt my cheeks grow hot and my body break into a sweat. What he'd said sounded like such a line, yet I reacted to it, mostly because it was true. Pathetic! Still, I summoned my pride and asked, "That's a joke, right?"

"You tell me," he murmured.

My inner self rolled her eyes to keep from falling for this crap. I stood up and put both hands on the table. I leaned close to get right in his face (which he didn't seem to mind).

"There is not now, nor will there ever be, any 'chemistry' between us, comprende?" I said through gritted teeth.

I didn't like doing this, but I had to. I couldn't let us get involved with each other. It seemed like the only way to get him away from me was to blow him off—ruthlessly.

I picked up my things and began to walk away, but not before I heard him say, "We'll see, Alexis … we will see." I turned back to shoot him an evil look and saw that he was leaning back on the bench, watching me with a hint of wonder in his eyes and a soft grin on his face.

I stormed off to my next class.

"*You're falling for him…*" the voice crooned.

I thought you had to go away for a while. What happened to that?

Chapter 15

It… was… INCREDIBLE! The house smelled of fresh paint, and the light-colored wood gleamed with gloss and shine. Everything about the space was beautiful; nothing seemed out of place! All the rooms had plenty of space but weren't too empty. The house was open and welcoming, but it also offered privacy. It gave off a sense of perfect harmony. It felt so… warm and bright. It felt like home.

"Mom, it's beautiful!" I exclaimed, surprised at my own enthusiasm. My mother looked over at me and smiled. She seemed happy, but something was off…. Her eyes didn't match the rest of her expression. She looked—

"How in the world were you able to find this place?" Dr. S. asked in amazement.

My mom let out a guilty little laugh. "Actually, I've had this house for a few years," she said slowly and carefully, as if she was crossing a minefield instead of carrying on a conversation.

Both my mouth and Dr. Seymour's dropped open as we stared in disbelief.

"Whhaaaat??" I asked.

"When… how… WHY?" Dr. Seymour stammered.

My mom grinned and said, "To be honest, I started working on this place right after we got to Tennessee. I wasn't sure if or when we would have to move again, so I bought this property and designed the house for it. Over the years, I saved up a little here and a little there and slowly had it built."

I couldn't believe it. My mother—she kept you guessing.

"Is there anything else you'd like to share with us?" Dr. S. asked sarcastically.

My mom laughed. "No, that's it… for now." She made a face and walked into the sunroom to unpack.

I looked over at Dr. Seymour, who shrugged. It seemed to be his shorthand for saying, "It's her world; we're just living in it."

I rolled my eyes and decided to go outside to check out the rest of the place.

☙

My mom had also forgotten to mention that the property was more than thirty acres, including a pool, a run-down barn, and a huge expanse of grass, surrounded by a big black fence.

The grass felt different in Florida. Up in Tennessee, it was soft and inviting, just begging you to lie down and count the stars. Here, it was itchy and thick, not at all roll-around–worthy. It would take some getting used to.

When I scanned the property line, I noticed that most of it backed up into a small forest, with young trees. I'd have to make a note of that. After I had surveyed the lawn, I walked to the back of the property, where the old barn stood.

Paranormal stuff didn't usually interest me or bug me too much, but this place gave me the creeps. I felt like someone was following me, which made me look over my shoulder every ten seconds or so. Every creak in the old wood made my heart stop. Every nerve in my body was on high alert.

After a few minutes of high-adrenaline pseudo–ghost hunting, I went back to the house.

Make that *ran* back to the house. In fact, I ran like hell back to the safe, warm house.

I opened the glass doors that looked out over the pool and found Mom and Dr. Seymour setting up the living room.

"Hey, so which one's my room?" I asked, interrupting their conversation.

They looked up from what they were doing, and my mom pointed upstairs.

"Pick whichever one you want; there's three to choose from."

As I walked upstairs, an eerie, déjà vu–type feeling washed over me. I felt as if I knew this house already or had seen it sometime before.

I shook the thought away and concentrated on picking my room. I finally chose the biggest of the three, although it was smaller than the master bedroom downstairs. The room was spacey and airy. I didn't feel trapped, which was vital to my sanity. The white, unsoiled carpet was soft and heavenly under my tired, itchy feet.

I marveled again at the fact that my mother had designed this house years earlier, then when back downstairs to help unpack.

ଓ

The moving van creeps arrived and left a few annoying hours later. It was a good thing they were gone, too, because my mom and I had been ready to kill them. (Of course, coming from me, that threat was more literal than it was from my mother, but I had managed to contain myself.)

It's not that we generally have anything against moving guys, but my mom caught some of the stuff they were thinking and… let's just say that both of us were a little creeped out. Actually, for me, the feeling was more along the lines of furiously ready to rip their heads off. But again, I remained calm.

After they left, I was finally able to relax. I sank my tired body down on the light beige sofa, lay my head on a soft, comforting pillow, and slowly let my heavy eyelids shut.

"Alexis, go get your room organized and then we'll order some pizza or something."

The nap had been nice while it lasted.

I groaned and received a glare from my mother. Then I made my way upstairs and began sorting my things.

It took a little while, but I finished. My bed was made, and my clothes were put away in the dresser. I arranged my desk and lined up my books on a small shelf. Then I gave myself a mental pat on the back for putting the effort into organizing.

I took a step back and admired my new room. As I glanced around to make sure everything was in place, I was suddenly hit with an overwhelming sensation.

My body froze while my mind started spinning. I caught my breath, and my heart stopped beating for a second. I stared blankly into space as I tried to slow down my thoughts.

Flashbacks were bouncing around my brain at the speed of light.

"The dream…" I breathed.

Of course! Why hadn't I realized it before?! Now, I knew why I'd had that feeling of déjà vu; I had seen this house before!

"Good! You're starting to piece everything together! You're getting closer, Alexis."

"Closer to what?" I managed to ask.

But of course, the voice was gone, although its words played over and over in my mind. I was completely frozen in place, as if my feet were encased in cement instead of standing on carpet. I didn't feel anything physically, but my mind was fixated on the uncanny familiarity of the room. There were some minute differences between this house and the one from my dream—the one where Taylor told me about Florida—but it was evident that they were the same.

I was snapped back to reality by my mother calling from downstairs: "Lex, do you want pepperoni or cheese?"

"Uh, whichever. Don't care," I managed to shout back.

"If you're done up there, come down here and help out," she ordered. Without responding, I slowly made my way toward the stairs, still in shock.

Bits and pieces of my dreams were coming true, but the big picture was still dangerously vague. I felt like I was beginning to make sense of some of the images, but I was still missing important pieces.

How can you feel like you're getting closer to something but still painfully far away?

What if you don't exactly *know* what and where you're getting closer to?

☙

"What do you think of the place now?" Dr. S. asked between bites.

I shrugged and said, "'S'okay, you know, if you're down with the whole 'haunted barn' thing." I gave him a look, and he opened his mouth, which was, of course, filled with chewed-up pizza. He let out a spooky "Ooooohhhh."

Real mature, Doc, real mature.

"Kent, come on," Mom said disapprovingly. He snickered and went back to eating. "What do you mean by haunted?" she asked, not seeming to get the joke.

"Ha, have you been out there recently? I took a tour and felt like a ghost was gonna jump out at me or something!" I said.

For some reason, Dr. S. found that hilarious, and I was soon laughing along with him. The exhaustion must have finally caught up to us.

My mom rolled her eyes and waited for us to return to sanity.

"Seriously, Mom, I really like the house. A lot," I said earnestly.

My mom smiled and said, "I'm glad."

For the first time in who knows how long, I felt calm. More than that, I was… happy. The fact that this house was the same one from my dream still gave me the chills, but I pushed the feeling aside. Everything that usually bothered me seemed to dissolve at that moment. Nothing fazed me. I had a sense of perfect tranquility.

But I was sure something would happen to make that feeling go bye-bye soon enough.

If a voice inside your head can sigh, mine did.

"*You're progressing,*" it said. "*Slowly... but at least you're progressing.*"

I mentally rolled my eyes and continued to enjoy the moment with Mom and Dr. S. I would deal with the voice and the dreams and anything else that came my way in the morning.

Chapter 16

"So anyway, she said that he said that *he* was just using *her* to get to her best friend!" Mandy went on, explaining another pointless bit of gossip to a girl named Lindsey.

"No!" Lindsey exclaimed with shock.

I rolled my eyes as I dug through my gym bag, looking for my clothes. I had been in the locker room for about ten minutes, and I had already heard three different stories about three different people who, apparently, didn't even go to our school.

"I know! And that's not even the worst part!" Mandy practically shouted as they finally walked out of the room. As I tried to calm myself down, I heard someone else enter the locker room.

"Oh, I don't think it can get any more painful than that!" Ariella said sarcastically, gesturing to the two who had just walked out.

"Seriously," I answered.

For the past few days, I had been growing more and more relaxed, especially around other people. I mean, I was still on my toes, and of course, most people still got on my nerves, but I was generally able to stay a lot calmer. I didn't feel like a ticking time bomb, which was... refreshing.

"Thank God they're gone; I was ready to smack Mandy!" Ariella said in a tone that I couldn't make out as either joking or serious.

"I thought you guys were all, like, friends?" I asked, confused.

I couldn't keep up with the whole clique thing here. I didn't really care that much about it, but still, if I was going to go to this school, I might as well know who hung out together.

"Eh, we're okay... more like really good acquaintances. We all just started hanging out together a few months ago," Ariella quickly explained.

"Oh, gotcha," I said flatly as I turned back to my bag, still trying to find my elusive gym clothes.

"So how're you doing around here? So far so good?" she asked casually. Without looking up, I answered.

"'S'all good, not too bad," I muttered as I rifled through my bag... for the hundredth time. I was starting to panic; class was going to start any minute and I couldn't find my gym clothes.

I know that forgetting my clothes wouldn't be the end of the world, but if you haven't figured out by now that even the slightest stressful situation can make me lose it, then you haven't been paying much attention.

If that's the case, then thanks a lot.

Even if I was getting better at saying under control, I still didn't trust myself.

I heard Ariella walk across the room and open a locker door. She rifled through some papers and other stuff before she closed the locker and came back to where I was standing.

"Here," she said, her outstretched hand holding some clothes.

I looked up at her, and she smiled. She waited patiently until I took the clothes.

"Um, thanks," I said with a hesitant grin as I changed into the loaned shirt and shorts.

"No problem," she said simply as she sat on the bench, waiting for me to finish. When I was ready, we both walked out… together.

☙

For gym class today, the coach had set up a game of field hockey for us to play. Knowing my own competitive side, I thought it would be a good idea not to participate too actively.

I sort of stood out of everyone's way and pretended to play whenever the coach looked up. I had been hovering on the edge of the game, watching some of the guys get *way* into it, when Sophia came up and stood next to me.

"I don't really feel like doing anything," she said. I smirked and watched as Evan and some other kid got into a fight over one of the rules of the game.

"Why do you think I'm over here?" I asked.

"Smart," she said lightly. I looked over at her and smiled.

For the next few minutes, we made casual small talk. You know: where we were from, what my last school was like, etc. It was all very natural and… ordinary. A few minutes later, Ariella come trotting up toward us. Her cheeks were flushed and her ponytail swished from side to side with each step she took.

"Is it just me, or is this not fun anymore?" she asked, motioning toward the same boys, who were apparently still arguing.

"Exactly why we're over here," Sophia said with a grin. I nodded my head in agreement.

We turned our attention back to the field to see Mandy attempting to settle the argument by… yelling at both of the boys?

How that was supposed to help, I had no idea.

"Let's just see how this all plays out, shall we?" Ariella said as she relaxed on the rough grass. I took a quick glance at Sophia, who was also getting comfortable on the ground.

I sat in between the two of them. We lounged in the extremely itchy grass while we waited for the rest of our class to finally settle down.

According to the coach, we had about ten more minutes of field time. Instead of going back to the others, the three of us spent our time trading lines from the funniest movies we had ever seen. By the end of the class, our sides were splitting from laughing so hard.

It turned out that we all had the same taste in films… go figure!

Sophia was rolling on the ground, Ariella's cheeks were streaked with tears, and my abs hurt like I had done a thousand crunches.

Even though my body was shaky and my head was light from laughing so hard, I was having… *fun*! In fact, this was the most fun I'd had in forever. I didn't want it to end. I wanted to stay out on that field forever, sitting in the grass (which I was actually getting used to), soaking up the Florida sun, and hanging out with some cool Normals.

Unfortunately, just a few short minutes later, the coach blew his whistle and motioned us to go inside to get changed.

Back in the locker room, I quickly changed into my school clothes and grabbed my stuff to head off to my next class.

"Ready?" I heard Sophia's voice ask from behind me.

I turned to see that she was waiting for me. I nodded as I picked up my backpack and started down the hall, following Sophia.

As we walked by the cafeteria, I saw May leaning against the wall. I turned my head to say hi, but her expression made my heart drop into my stomach.

She glowered at me with eyes that seemed to be emerald steel. I could practically feel the flames as her gaze burned into me. Her expression was painful to read, as if I had done something horribly wrong to her. But the thing that brought me to a halt was the fact that her eyes were glowing again. I couldn't get over the impression they made on me. They were… dangerously beautiful. I stared intently into her face while she scrutinized mine. For a moment, everything around me disappeared. All I could see was May's fierce, deadly, mystifying—

"Alexis? Are you coming?" Sophia's voice broke through the haze.

I tore my gaze away from May to look in her direction. Sophia stood a few feet ahead of me, waiting for me to continue walking to class.

Instead of looking back at May, which part of me really wanted to, I turned away and followed Sophia.

What in the world had just happened?

☙

"We should have that much fun in first period and lunch every day!" Ariella exclaimed as she put the last of her homework into her backpack. I looked up and saw Sophia nodding in agreement.

"Totally, that was awesome!" I responded with sincere enthusiasm, remembering the lunch I'd had with Sophia, Ariella, Mandy, Evan, and a few new kids I'd met. These people were absolutely hilarious!

The three of us shared a glance and a smile as we packed up the books we needed to go home.

"Sounds like you guys had fun in P.E.," Mandy said. I couldn't tell if she was being snarky or not. "Glad I was included."

Oh yeah, definitely snarky.

Ariella rolled her eyes and shut her locker door. I ignored the last part of Mandy's remark and answered, "Yeah, good times."

"Well, tomorrow, Mandy, come hang out with us. I mean, you could have come and sat with us today," Sophia said, trying to lessen the sudden awkwardness of the conversation.

Mandy let out a "humph" and shrugged her shoulders. Sophia, Ariella, and I all shared a look and ignored her minor temper tantrum.

After a minute, we all said goodbye, and Sophia and I made our way to the car line.

As soon as we got outside, I saw Mom in our black Suburban. Disappointed, I waved to Sophia as I climbed into the car.

As I settled into my seat, Mom drove out of the parking lot and onto the main road. I was turning on the air conditioning when I noticed that she was smiling and glancing over at me.

"What?" I said with a smile. She turned toward me and her face lit up.

"You had a good day," she replied happily. I shrugged and smiled a little bigger.

"It *was* good," I said, utterly genuine. My mom shifted her eyes back to the road in front of her and grinned. "Actually, it was amazing," I continued. "I made friends with that girl, Sophia. And I'm getting to know a lot of other people. All day I felt… I don't even know how to describe it," I said, reliving P.E. and lunch in my mind, my smile growing with each memory that flashed across my brain.

My mom reached one arm around me and gave me a gentle squeeze. "I'm so glad, Alexis," she said lovingly.

Now my smile was even *bigger*! My cheeks felt like they were about to explode.

But still, underneath my exhilaration, I had a feeling that something was wrong. Not just the whole thing with May, but something else… possibly *someone* else.

I mentally swatted the thought away, returning my mind to the laughs I'd shared with Sophia and Ariella during the field hockey game. What an awesome day! I didn't completely hate school and I had some friends. I wasn't going to let anything ruin that.

"*So the boogey man made some friends after all?*" I heard the voice snicker as it spoke. I got mad for a second, but then thought about what it had said.

I had made friends… me! Possibly the most dangerous living thing on this planet. Wasn't I the one who had said, time and time again, that all Normals were bad news and should be avoided at all costs? Now, I actually considered some of these frail people to be my friends.

I couldn't get over how naturally and willingly I had bonded with the girls at school. I wasn't sure whether I was beginning to trust my newfound control or just becoming careless. Regardless of the answer,

I was starting to get the feeling that maybe it wasn't so bad for me to be close to some Normals.

"*Maybe you aren't so different from these Normals...*" the voice said vaguely. As I thought about those words, it spoke again: "*Maybe you're more like them than you give yourself credit for.*"

Chapter 17

I hated nights like this one. I was exhausted and wanted to sleep, but my eyes refused to stay closed and my mind would not shut down. I had gone to bed around 10:00, the usual time, but I think I had been lying awake for three hours. It felt like more, but three hours was probably about right.

I couldn't tell whether I had fallen asleep and woken up or had never fall asleep in the first place, but either way, the night seemed never-ending.

Turning over to my other side—again—I stared out the window by my bed, overlooking the shadowy pool and the dark green lawn below. The window was exceptionally large and exceedingly wide and still had no curtains.

You would think that after a month of living in this house, we could have gotten some curtains for the windows, but no.

After a while, I gave up on the window and walked over to my white wooden desk. I opened my laptop and pushed the power button. The light of the screen blinded me at first, but my eyes got used to the sudden brightness. The opening tone of the computer cracked the brittle silence and the light melted the dense darkness of my room.

Once my laptop was up and running, I went straight to a saved file that I had created a couple of months ago, "Dreams." The file included a typed document and a couple of links for some Internet articles.

When I first started having the nightmares, I made a file on my computer so I could record them and try to analyze them later. I hoped that writing down what happened in the dreams might help me figure them out. I had also done some research on Native American culture to see if I could learn anything useful about the dream in which the Native American girl became me.

Even though it sounds all organized and manageable, let me tell you, it wasn't. So far, it was just a jumbled mess of ideas.

Taking a deep breath, I looked at my checklist of dreams. In this file, I'd listed everything I did and didn't know about each weird dream I'd had.

So far, one dream had come completely true, the one about Florida. Taylor was in Florida; I was living in the same house as the one in my dream; my eyes had developed the spooky white ring; and the black fog was apparently still in my head.

The dream in which I had shattered Taylor's face had partially come true. I had seen the two trees from that dream in the forest in Tennessee, but I didn't know who the shadowy figure was, and Taylor's face was still intact.

That dream terrified me, especially now that I knew where Taylor was living. If my dreams were really visions of the future, then did that one mean that I was going to kill Taylor? In the dream, I had shattered him, which must be the equivalent of crushing him. Just like I had done to—

I glanced down at my purse sitting on the floor, where I'd stashed the folded piece of paper that was Andy's note—still unread.

My entire body shivered as I turned back to my laptop. With shaky fingers, I read down to the next page of the document to look at the last dream: the Native American one.

I still had no freaking clue what that one meant. As far as I could see, this dream was the only one that proved I wasn't having visions because, frankly, I didn't think I was suddenly going to become a scary Native American hunter.

My face dropped into my palms as I closed my eyes, trying to make sense of the images. I could feel a major headache coming on.

After a minute, I clicked on one of the links in the Dreams folder. It led to a Web site I had found that was filled with information on traditions, religions, and other cool stuff about Native Americans.

Once the page loaded, I clicked on a link labeled "Native American symbolism." It seemed that there were underlying meanings for *everything*, including the sun, the sky, and the grass.

I immediately started searching for anything that had to do with my dream. After twenty minutes of reading, I'd had no luck. I was almost ready to give up, when a line of bold green print caught my eye. It said: **"THE COYOTE."**

My heart raced and my hands started twitching and sweating. Holding my breath, I clicked the link.

THE COYOTE:

Coyote was a popular spirit among western tribes. He was a sly trickster, but he also made life interesting for people. Coyote was also responsible for sorrow and death.

I sat and stared blankly at the article lighting up my laptop's screen. Images of the little coyote from my nightmare raced through my head. The sudden understanding that hit me was almost enough to make me faint: Sand-colored fur, baby-blue eyes, troublemaker… Andy.

And—oh my gosh—*death.* If my dreams were visions, did that mean Andy would never come out of his coma?

"Life does not hand us the answers we need. We must unravel the meaning of our lives and find our own destiny."

The voice really needed to quit with the trippy "Confucius say" crap. It was scaring me.

ᘓ

"Alexis?" a voice said, shattering my trance. I looked up from the stone patio of the outdoor eating area at school to see Sophia, Mandy, and Ariella staring at me.

"What? Sorry," I said, surprised. Sophia was examining me, probably wondering why I was so out of it, while Mandy rolled her eyes.

"We were planning to go to the beach over spring break," Ariella explained patiently. "You in?"

"Oh, yeah, sounds good. I'll ask my mom about it," I said, regaining my composure. Ariella smiled and went back to talking to Evan. Sophia joined their conversation, but Mandy continued to stare at me. She had been giving me the eye all day, though I didn't know why.

"What?" I finally asked, irritated.

"You look like a zombie," she said with a smirk. I grimaced and she laughed.

"You okay?" a deep voice asked from the other side of the table. It was Tom, one of my other new Normal friends. "You do look kind of rough."

The icy blue of his eyes seemed even more remarkable paired with his dark, chocolate-colored hair. He had just taken off his black football sweatshirt and was now wearing a dark blue JCS polo.

"Yeah, I just didn't get much sleep last night," I said, smiling slightly. He returned the smile and went back to talking to the others.

I played with my lunch for a few minutes until I had the sudden feeling that someone was staring at me. I looked up to see that the feeling was right; someone *was* watching me.

His dark, impenetrable eyes shifted casually back and forth from me to… whoever he was talking to. He was sitting with a brown-haired girl, but I couldn't tell who she was until she got up from her bench to throw something away. As she turned away from the garbage can, her scowling jade gaze met my eyes.

May. It figured….

Just this past week, Taylor and May had suddenly become friends. They sat together at lunch and talked in the halls, and she flirted with him constantly. I couldn't figure out what was going on between them.

Not that I cared or anything….

A voice from my table threw off my train of thought and made my heart stop momentarily.

"What's with the death glare?" Will asked. I yanked my eyes away from the two annoying lovebirds and looked at Will's hazel eyes and pale face. "You look like you're ready to punch someone," he said lightheartedly.

"Just drifting off into space again," I said with a weak smile and a voice to match. He smiled and flipped his red hair out of his eyes as he turned back to the others.

I let out a short, angry breath as I involuntarily turned my attention back to Taylor and May. Taylor was now fully focused on May, who was laughing WAY too loud at something that probably wasn't even funny.

I couldn't believe I had even considered being friends with that girl. Just looking at her made my blood boil and my hands clench into angry fists. Even thinking or saying her name felt like acid running down my throat. I hated her. I hated *him* for even associating with her!

"*I thought you didn't care,*" the voice said, an edge in its tone. My jaw clenched and I felt myself blush.

I don't, I thought shortly. I heard the voice let out an irritated huff of breath, then go silent.

I had gotten so wrapped up in my hatred for May and Taylor that I forgot I was staring. He turned his eyes away from *her* and looked at me.

I quickly jerked my head away from him and pretended to be wrapped up in the group's conversation. I snuck a peak out of the corner of my eye and could have sworn I saw him smirk and roll his eyes.

Smooth move on my part.

❧

The sun wasn't even up yet as I entered the school. The hallway was lit only by a couple of eerie, flickering lights, and I could barely see the numbers of the combination dial on my locker.

I was here earlier than usual because my mom was sick and Dr. S. had offered to take me to school on his way to the hospital. Make that *half an hour* earlier than usual.

Note to self: Torture Doc first chance I got.

I put all my books away once I *finally* got my locker open (fourth time's a charm), and I even took the time to organize my binders. That left me with just twenty-five minutes to spend in the deserted hall with nothing to do. I slumped to the floor and started playing with my phone.

A few quiet minutes passed before I heard footsteps approaching from around the corner. Thinking it was a teacher, I stuffed my phone back into my purse and jumped up, trying to look innocent.

I couldn't see exactly who was coming up the hallway, but I knew from the backpack that it wasn't a teacher, so I relaxed a little. I tried to force my eyes to peer through the darkness but then realized that I must have looked like an idiot to whoever was heading my way.

I turned and tried to open my locker again, covering up my own awkwardness. The person at the end of the hall had stopped at a locker, put some stuff away, and shut the door. He stood leaning against the wall for a few seconds, then walked toward me.

I tried to focus on getting my locker open and not on how much I looked like a loser for hanging around in the hallway alone before school, but with each step he took, I grew more and more flustered. When the footsteps stopped a few feet from me, I finally looked up.

Of course, it was Taylor.

My shoulders and back tightened, and my hands grew shakier. He leaned his shoulder up against the locker next to mine and said, "Having trouble?"

"Nope," I answered, looking down and fumbling with the lock. My jaw was clenched and my voice was tense when I spoke. He stayed where he was for a second, watching me struggle, then reached into his pocket. He pulled something out and I heard it open. Suddenly, a little light shone on my locker, illuminating the numbers perfectly.

I looked up and saw that Taylor had pulled out his cell phone and was casting the backlight of it onto the combination dial. His features were barely visible, but I could still see the dark silhouette of his perfect body and the outlines of his face.

God, he was gorgeous… even in the dark.

I looked down again, now blushing, and opened my locker with ease. I stuck my purse in the locker and closed the door.

"Um, thanks," I said shyly, still not daring to look him straight in the face.

"No problem," he said simply as he put his phone back in his pocket.

The light was beginning to come into the hallway, and it was easier to see. A few other students slowly trickled in.

After a long, awkward moment, Taylor spoke: "Have you thought about what I said?" he asked, so coolly and calmly that, at first, I had no idea what he was talking about. After a second, his meaning came to me like a speeding boomerang—his theory about our "chemistry."

I put on my best "tough girl" face and looked fiercely into his eyes. My toughness faltered a little when I saw the gentleness there, and my heart fluttered at his grin, but I hoped I hadn't given too much away.

"You're not exactly one to beat around the bush, huh?" I asked.

He shrugged modestly in response. I felt myself start to smile, but I chomped down on the inside of my cheek to stop it. I kept my gaze hard and spoke carefully.

"I gave you my answer. It hasn't changed." He looked away from me for a second, as if he was thinking.

Then, he snickered softly and shook his head, letting some of his black hair fall in front of one of his eyes. With a determined look on his face, he took a step closer to me. I didn't back away.

"I don't think your answer was the truth," he said, still holding me in his eyes.

"Oh yeah?" I asked, half mockingly.

"Yeah, I think you've had a thing for me since that first time you ran into me," he said smugly, his mouth turning back into a crooked grin as he raised one eyebrow.

Immediately, my face burned fiery hot, and the electrical circuits in my brain shorted out. I couldn't think of *anything* to say to that because:

A) I was completely mortified,

B) I was trying to refrain from calling him a jerk, and

C) What he said might be true.

"You don't know anything," I fired back.

"I beg to differ," he said calmly, sliding in closer to me. My nerve endings simmered with uncertainty and the beginnings of rage. The hallways and the other students around me seemed to fade; everything dimmed, except for Taylor.

We were so close that I could easily reach out and touch his face. He slowly leaned in closer, his black hair falling over his dark, enticing eyes, his face now almost close enough to—

"Taylor," a voice said sternly from right next to us. We both jumped and turned to see May standing in the hall.

Boy, did she look ticked off.

"What's going on?" she asked with a sharp edge in her voice. She glared at Taylor with her emerald scowl, and he seemed to be lost in her eyes, which were lit up again by that eerie glow.

Who exactly did she think she was? This girl was asking for a good butt-kicking.

Taylor looked back at me apologetically and answered. "Just helping Alexis with her locker," he said, as if our whole conversation had never happened. My jaw clenched.

What a jerk! Both of them! I didn't know who I hated more right then, Taylor or May. It was obvious that they were into each other, but if Taylor was so into May, then why was he trying to *kiss* me? He seemed to like me, but he changed every time *she* came around. Did he even care that I liked him?

"*Finally! You're improving so much, Alexis!*" the voice exclaimed. I was thrown off by the sudden excitement in its tone, then realized what it was talking about.

"Well," May finally said. "Okay then." She turned away from Taylor and stormed off. He watched her walk away, then turned back toward me.

"Look, Alexis," he started, but I turned around and started walking away. Feeling tears swim into my eyes, I tried to get as far away from him as possible, but he caught up to me and touched my shoulder.

I wanted to pull away, but I couldn't get my body to listen. He walked around to face me, still keeping one hand on my shoulder.

"I really think there's something special between us. I wouldn't be trying so hard to talk to you if I didn't believe that," he said softly. I looked down, swallowed the urge to whimper, and replaced my sadness with anger.

"Oh, yeah, you're trying *so hard*," I began sarcastically, my voice growing stronger with each word I said. I shoved his hand off me as I continued. "You really want me to believe that ignoring me for a month is trying?" I asked, rage flooding my words. He stood up straighter and stared at me, his eyes suddenly darker and dangerous-looking.

"Oh, I'm the one to blame?" he asked, sounding just as angry as I did. "You're the one who's been doing everything in your power to avoid me," he said, trying to put the blame on me.

"Why do you care anyway? It looks like you and May are doing quite nicely." My voice dropped down a notch but was still hard as a rock. Taylor's eyes went wide and his face became still. He seemed staggered by my statement.

I won't lie: It felt pretty good to catch him like that. But I also felt like crap. He was confusing me. One second, it seemed that he really liked me—I mean, he tried to kiss me—but when May showed up and I confronted him about her, he didn't have anything to say.

I really wanted to curl up into a ball and cry, but I couldn't let that show. Without another word, I turned around and walked down the hallway. He let me go without a fight.

"*He really does care about you*," the voice said sincerely. I rolled my eyes and shook my head. "*And you feel the same way...*" it continued, stating what I knew to be a fact.

That doesn't mean we can be together, I thought with sorrow, as I looked back and saw him, standing alone in the hall, the other students flowing around him.

Chapter 18

The rest of the day couldn't have gone by any slower! I was pretty sure I would completely and totally lose it before the last bell rang. Listening to the teachers plod through their material felt like pulling out my hair, piece by painful piece. But thank God, my last class was almost over. I just had to survive ten more—

"Hey, what happened this morning?" Sophia asked softly as soon as Mrs. Drake let us talk.

"What do you mean?" I replied, feeling weak and tired.

"I saw you talking to Taylor; it looked like you guys were fighting or something," she said. I dropped my gaze to the floor, trying to fight back fresh tears. "And pretty much all day," she continued, "you've looked like you wanted to cry."

I kept my face away from hers as I tried to regain some control.

"It's... kind of a long story," I said, my voice quivering. Sophia looked at me, no doubt anticipating that I would tell it. "I… don't really want to talk about it," I said as gently as I could.

"Oh, okay. I understand… I guess. But just in case, here's my number," she said as she took out a piece of paper and a pen. "Call me if you need anything, okay?" she said with a smile. Her kind gesture made me feel a lot better.

Over the past week or so, I'd discovered that having Normal friends was really nice. I'd almost forgotten why I hated the idea so much in the first place… almost. I was still aware of the dangers posed by my powers, and I knew that losing control was always a possibility, but I think I trusted myself enough to open up a little bit.

"*A little trust never hurt anyone,*" the voice said encouragingly. .

I smiled at Sophia as she wrapped her arms around me, and I returned the hug, very carefully, of course.

"Thanks," I said appreciatively. She let go and gave me a big smile.

"All right, class," Mrs. Drake announced, "you're dismissed. Have a good afternoon! Only two more days to go!" she added, referring to spring break next week.

As we packed up our things and headed toward the door, Sophia asked, "Did you talk to your mom about the beach?"

"Yeah, she said it was cool," I replied, remembering the talk I'd had with my mom the previous night. "She also said you guys could come over and spend the night now that we're settled in."

"Yeah, let's do it! I'll ask tonight and text you," Sophia said excitedly as she walked out the classroom door. I smiled and followed her, more than ready to go home.

As I was taking books out of my locker, I texted my mom to see if Doc would be taking me home today. Her response: "Yes, but he won't be there for another half an hour."

Crap.

I forcefully slammed my locker door and let out an irritated "UGH!" receiving a couple of weird looks and almost breaking my locker in the process.

"Alexis, what's wrong?" I heard a voice ask from behind me. I turned around to see Ariella and Mandy in their soccer warm-ups.

"Oh, it's just my mom's…" I started to answer but stopped.

I had no idea what to call Doc! Was he officially my mom's boyfriend? If so, would that sound weird to my new friends? Should I just say he's a friend, or was that the same thing as saying he was her boyfriend?

"I mean, err… my… my stepdad…"

Eh, sounded weird, but it worked.

"My mom's sick, but he's not coming to get me for another half an hour," I said, trying to regain some poise.

Ariella looked at me suspiciously, but Mandy didn't seem to notice my discomfort.

"We don't have practice for another hour, so just come hang out with us," Mandy offered.

"Sure," I said, still sounding a little distant. I slung my backpack over my shoulder and followed both of them to the outdoor eating area, where most of the team was hanging out. Mandy went off to talk to some other girls who were on the team, but Ariella sat down at an empty wooden table. I followed slowly behind and sat on the bench across from Ariella.

We talked casually for a few minutes, about school, plans for spring break, and some other stuff.

"Can I ask you something?" she said with a half smile.

I froze for a second, feeling my heart rate speed up. I swallowed hard and said, "Uh, sure… what's up?"

She took a short breath and blurted, "Do you like Taylor?"

I hadn't seen that coming. Her question totally caught me off guard. Without even thinking, I muttered, "Yes."

"Ah! I knew it!" she said, beaming.

"Why do you ask?" I was afraid that someone might have started a stupid rumor about us.

"*It can't be a rumor if it's true,*" the voice said, sounding almost as if it was smiling (if that was even possible). I tried to think of a witty comeback, but Ariella interrupted my internal conversation.

"I just knew," she said, still sort of bouncing around. She saw the look of confusion on my face and continued. "I have a good eye for this kind of stuff. I can always tell when people like each other or if two people would be good together," she quickly clarified.

"Oh," I said absently. I was still in a minor state of shock. Was it that obvious that we liked each other? I knew *I* liked *him*, but the question remained whether he really liked me. It was hard to tell with all the mixed signals he was giving me.

"You guys would be so cute together!" Ariella went on. "I mean, I haven't known you very long, but I know a good couple when I see one!"

"Yeah, well, he needs to get that memo," I mumbled.

"Why? What's wrong?" she asked sincerely.

Damn it. Why did I have to run my big mouth? I needed to remember to keep some emotions to myself.

I let out a sigh and prepared to vent: "I can't tell if he really likes me or not."

"Explain," she said.

"Just this morning, he came up to me before school and said that he knows I like him. Then he leaned in to kiss me—"

"He kissed you?!" Ariella exclaimed excitedly.

"SHH!" I hissed as I looked around, making sure no one had heard her. "No, he *almost* did," I corrected.

"Still counts!" she joked. I grimaced at her and she laughed. "Okay, go on."

"Anyway, he almost kissed me, but then May showed up," I said, my muscles tensing at the memory.

"Figures," she said sourly as she rolled her eyes.

"Then she asked what was going on, and Taylor said he was just 'helping me with my locker,'" I said, making air quotes with my fingers.

"What a jerk," Ariella said.

"I know! Then I called him out on it, and he got this look like a deer in headlights!"

I was shaking now. Just thinking about this morning made my blood boil, but actually talking about it made me even more furious at Taylor. My fists were so tightly balled up that my knuckles turned white and my fingers went numb.

"You know," Ariella began, "Taylor had no excuse for acting like that, but the whole thing is more May's fault than his."

I focused on keeping my cool as Ariella continued.

"She bounces around to a new guy every week; Taylor is just another boy toy she'll soon get bored with. But she does have a weird effect on guys; it's like she hypnotizes them or something. All the guys fall for it—I have yet to see one that hasn't—so don't worry about Taylor being a total jerk. I'm sure that's not what he's really like."

Everything Ariella said seemed to make sense. Yes, Taylor still had some explaining to do, but it was mostly May. The more I thought about it, the less tense I felt.

I lifted my heavy gaze from the ground and looked at Ariella with appreciation.

"You think?" I asked.

"Definitely, and don't worry about whether he likes you or not. Because he does."

"How do you know?" There was no way she could know that for a fact—unless Taylor told her. Which wouldn't make sense, because they don't even hang out.

"Like I said, I haven't known him long, so I could be wrong. But in the short time he's been here, I've seen how he acts around people. Taylor doesn't really care that much about what people do or what they think about him. Like, he doesn't get caught up in high school stuff. When he first came here, almost every girl was begging for his attention, but he just couldn't care less. But when you came here, I don't know. Something was different about him. He's always looking at you and acts like he really wants to talk to you. It's almost like you're the only girl he sees here."

I smiled as she spoke. Sure, the whole thing with May was confusing, but hearing that Ariella noticed Taylor's interest in me made up for that little episode.

"Thanks, that really helps." Just as I spoke, I felt my phone vibrate inside my purse. I unzipped it and looked to see that Doc was calling. "Hold on a sec," I said to Ariella as I answered the phone.

"Hello?"

"Hey, I'm on my way to the school, but I had to make a quick stop at the store. I'll call you back when I'm pulling into the parking lot," Doc said from the other end of the line.

"Okay, thanks," I replied. I looked over at Ariella and said, "I have to go. My… err… stepdad is almost here."

"Okay, text you later," she said as I walked away.

"Bye!" I called over my shoulder, making my way back through the school to the car line out front. As I rounded the corner to the entrance of the main hallway, I saw Taylor and May together.

I stopped and slowly retreated to a spot where they couldn't see me. Still holding my phone in my hand, I tried to sneak a look at what they were up to.

I swear, I'm not a stalker.

Taylor was at his locker, putting books away, while May stood behind him. She twirled and flipped her hair as she yapped away, looking at him with hungry eyes and a smirk on her face.

I rolled my eyes at how hard she was trying. Did she really think he was going to fall for her Little Miss Cutesy act? I laughed a little to myself when Taylor didn't even bother to turn around, but then... OMG.

Taylor did turn around, and when he did, May threw her boney little arms around his neck and smashed her mouth onto his. She held him in a death grip, pushing her body as close to his as possible.

My jaw almost hit the floor—and so did my phone—at what I saw next. Not only did May have the nerve to kiss him, but he was kissing her back! I waited for him to pull away, but instead, he put his hands lightly on her hips and tilted his head more to the side, finding the perfect angle for the kiss.

I am going to kill her. Oh, she's done it now! Just wait until I catch her alone...

My phone vibrated, and I flipped it open but was too stunned to speak. "Alexis? You there, kid?" I heard Doc's voice ask.

My hands shook violently, and my arms and legs went completely numb. My teeth were gritted so hard that I wouldn't be surprised if I cracked a few molars.

"Alexis?" Doc repeated, trying to get my attention.

My feet refused to move, but my mind was filled with thoughts of deliciously murderous revenge. I tried to regain control, but I couldn't. I had to get away from the school before I hurt someone, but the nearest and safest exit was through the doors at the other end of the hall—I would have to go past the make-out scene.

That would be a little awkward…

Finally, I lifted the phone to my ear and spoke to Doc. "I… something's wrong," I began in a tense and strained voice. "Angry, running, be home later." Without waiting for a reply, I hung up and shoved the cell phone into my purse.

I took a deep breath and held it as I spun around the corner and began power-walking toward the exit. The hallway wasn't that long, but the door seemed to be a bazillion miles away.

Right before I passed the lovebirds, Taylor broke the kiss with May and saw me. I met his gaze for half a second but quickly looked away and walked even faster.

It took every ounce of control I had to keep from reaching out and snapping May's skinny little neck. It would've been easy, too; she was right beside me. But I ignored the violent thoughts and kept going.

"Alexis," Taylor said as he pulled away from May, but I was already at the end of the hall. I forced the doors open and, as soon as I was outside, began running as fast as my legs would carry me—not caring who saw.

In the space of about ten seconds, I accelerated from twenty to *two hundred* miles an hour. The city of Jacksonville flashed by me at top speed. My tear-filled eyes burned from the wind and my face felt like it was on fire.

I didn't know exactly where I was going, but all I really cared about was putting distance between myself and Taylor… and May… and anything else that was making my life miserable or complicated. I wanted to be away from it all. I wanted to run until I couldn't run anymore.

"*You can't hide from your problems, Alexis,*" the voice said calmly.

"*No, but I sure as hell can try.*" With that thought, I pushed myself to sprint even faster.

The rush from my speed was intoxicating. I had never felt anything like *this* before. I wasn't even winded. Everything around me became a blur of blended color. I glanced down at my legs to see how fast they were pumping, then let my head fall back and let out an almost maniacal laugh.

I could've kept up this pace all day. I wanted to keep it up forever.

Chapter 19

A cool but comfortable breeze tickled my senses as I slowly woke up. Without opening my eyes, I knew that I was outside. I could feel the lightness of the air and the sun warming my skin.

I moved carefully, conscious of the aches and pains in my neck and head. I gently stretched my arms and felt soft grass glide under my grimy skin. A familiar scent filled my nostrils: pine needles and mountain air.

After a minute, I reluctantly opened my eyes. I had to blink hard a few times to get them clear and moist again. When I finally saw where I was, my dry mouth dropped like a dead weight.

I was in a forest—at least, what was left of one. All the trees around me either had big holes in them or were snapped in half. The only trees left standing looked to be about a quarter of a mile away. Even the ground was destroyed! There were craters everywhere, each about four or five feet deep, and the grass was torn to shreds. The spot I had been lying in looked to be the only area left intact.

What had I done?

I looked down and saw that my school uniform was ruined. My skirt had been torn in several places and my shirt was stained with grass, dirt, and dried blood—which I hoped was *my* blood.

I stood up—wincing in pain—and checked my body for any serious damage. I had one or two good cuts on my arms, but other than that, just a couple of scrapes and bruises and, apparently, soreness.

I was stunned by the devastation I'd apparently caused in the forest, and I knew I had to find my way home before someone else came along and saw my handiwork. But first, I had to figure out where I was.

BZZZZZZ! BZZZZZZ!

I jumped and yelped at the vibration of my phone. I looked down and saw my backpack and purse lying on the ground next to my feet.

Breathing deeply, I picked up my purse and reached in for my phone. My movements were slow to compensate for the insane headache I was experiencing, so when I finally got a hold of the phone, I had missed the call.

It was my mom, apparently calling for the thirty-seventh time. How long had I been gone?

I quickly punched in her number and waited until she picked up.

"Alexis! Thank God! Where are you? Are you okay? What happened?" my mom asked, barely taking a breath between sentences.

"Yeah, I'm okay, Mom," I said. I cleared my throat before continuing. "I don't know where I am though."

"How could you *not* know?" my mother asked, shocked by my statement.

"How *could* I know?! I don't remember anything!" There was a moment of silence between us.

I glanced at the ground and saw a folded piece of paper. It must have fallen out of my purse.

"You don't remember where you are or how you got there?" my mother finally asked.

I reached down and picked up the dirty, wrinkled paper as I answered. "No, not a clue. But I can take a wild guess and say that I was *really* pissed off," I said sarcastically. As I studied the paper, my mom responded.

"Why? Are you in a forest?"

"What's left of one, yes."

"How bad?" she asked simply.

"On a scale of one to ten…" I looked up and scanned the ruined area as I answered, "I'd say twelve and a half."

I looked back down at the paper, turning and twisting it as I tried to open it one-handed.

"We'll deal with that later… Listen, you need to find out where you are and come home immediately," she commanded.

Her tone made my aching muscles tighten. No teenager responds well to a direct order.

I was about to fire a comeback at her, when I finally got the paper open and saw the name signed at the bottom.

Oh yeah, I remembered stashing that in my purse before we moved.

Feeling my heart thud nervously against my rib cage, I answered my mom.

"Okay, I'll call you when I know where I am."

"Thank you. And be safe, Lex. I love you," she said. God, she sounded like she was never going to see me again.

Taking a deep breath, I answered, "Love you, too, Mom."

I slid the phone back into my purse, feeling my heart drop into my stomach and my throat close tightly as I focused my attention on the ruined piece of paper in my hand.

"*You're ready,*" the voice said reassuringly.

I closed my eyes and nodded as I opened the paper and prepared myself for the worst.

Alexis-

Hear me out. I'm not here to give you a hard time. I actually need you to read this very carefully and think about every word I write. You may choose to believe me or not, but I think you deserve a fair warning. Okay, here goes:

You and your mom aren't alone. YOU aren't alone. Your abilities weren't given to you as a curse. They are the exact opposite. You have a destiny, a role, a purpose. You already know what it is, but you haven't realized it yet.

Not everyone you meet will be who they say they are. More than one person will deceive you, and if you do not learn from the experience, there will be more. More lies and more hurt for you and those you love.

I'm sorry I have to be so vague, but it's the only way I can help without interfering too much. You have much more to learn and more mysteries to solve. You will have to step in to stop more than one conspiracy. You'll have to figure most of this out on your own, but I hope this note will help you a little when you read it in the future.

Yours always,

Andy

I must have reread the note twenty times

How in God's beautiful green earth did that annoying kid know about my curse? How did he know about my mom's powers? Conspiracies… what did he mean by that?

The note was completely mind-blowing.

My head throbbed so intensely that I couldn't even think straight. I shoved the note back into my purse and slung my bag over my shoulder. I picked up my phone and went to the GPS application, praying that it could show me where I was.

After a few minutes, a map popped up. Great, the stupid GPS seemed to think I still lived in Chattanooga.

Stamping my foot and groaning in frustration, I threw the phone back into my purse and took off running.

My legs shrieked with pain, and I thought I could actually feel my skull splitting, but I kept going.

I didn't exactly know where I was heading, but anything was better than just standing around in the ruined forest.

"*Go left.*"

Without questioning the voice, I made an immediate left turn. As I ran, the forest around me began to look less like the aftermath of a hurricane. I sped past large, lush trees and ran through thick, welcoming grass. After a few minutes, I heard cars in the distance. Ignoring my screaming muscles, I picked up the pace and finally broke through the woods.

I discovered a small, aged road, surrounded by older houses and a few small shops. It looked like one of those historic main streets that most towns no longer had.

I checked my surroundings, looking for some kind of landmark. I didn't see any helpful signs that read "Welcome to…."

Taking a short breath, I decided to go into one of the stores and ask for directions. The nearest one was called "Marion's Used Books." Maybe "Marion" could tell me where the heck I was.

The old, wooden door creaked, and the smell of dank carpet and dusty paper tickled my nose.

The place had looked much bigger from the outside. When I entered, I saw only about five dark shelves filled with worn books and two old couches, leftovers from the seventies. A dingy carpeted staircase led to the second floor. The cashier's desk was right next to the front door. It held a computer, an old family photo, and a little bell on the ledge.

I rang the little bell twice.

No response.

I tapped the bell once more and heard someone call from upstairs.

"I'm comin'!" an old, hoarse voice growled angrily. An elderly man made his way slowly down the stairs.

He looked like the kind of grumpy geezer that took pleasure in other people's misery. He was completely bald and wore glasses. His pants were belted up around his armpits and he wore a pair of faded green slippers.

"Whatta yah want, huh?" he grumbled. I assumed this was Mr. Marion.

"Um, I was wondering if I could get some directions," I answered politely.

"Hmph, I couldn't give yah directions farther than this here town," he said in a thick accent.

Patiently, I answered, "That's okay; I just need to know where I am now."

He looked me up and down and said, "Whatta yah, runnin' from the law or sumthin'? I won't be havin' no fugitives in mah store, young lady."

"Will you *please* tell me the name of the town I'm in?" I asked through gritted teeth, my patience finally cracking.

He straightened himself up and walked over to the cashier's counter. "Nope," he said without looking at me.

"Look— " I started, but his jaw tightened, and he interrupted me.

"You best get outta here, or I'll call the cops," he said threateningly.

I felt my hands ball up and my tender shoulders tense. Taking in a deep breath, I spun on my heels and reached for the doorknob, but a photo tacked to the back of the door stopped me.

The picture was of a boy, about eight or nine years old. He had light blonde hair and baby blue eyes. He looked just like—

"Um, is this… your grandson?" I asked, catching the old guy before he walked away.

"Him? No… no, he isn't," he said, his voice suddenly tight. I looked back at the picture, not fully believing what I saw. Could it be?

"What's his name?"

"That's Andrew," the old man said carefully. He stood next to me now, staring at the picture. I glanced over at him and was surprised to see tears falling down his cheeks. "His ma and me adopted him when he was a baby."

There was a moment of silence before I spoke.

"Something happened to him?" Mr. Marion nodded but didn't look at me.

"He was hit by a car and put into a deep coma a couple months ago. Andrew was on his way to school when it happened… was his first day of real school, too. The boy was homeschooled all his life but finally convinced me and his ma to let him go." As he spoke, his voice shook, and he had to swallow hard to regain control.

I could feel tears beginning to flow down my own dirty cheeks.

Mr. Marion looked at me appreciatively. "You know, he's a strange one," he said with a playful tone. "Always talkin' about how he would soon 'fulfill his destiny.' I never could figure that boy out." He paused as his face grew serious. "Come to think of it… the day he left for school, he was talkin' all sorts of nonsense, somethin' about helpin' someone else start on the road to their destiny. He said that his duty was calling, and he couldn't ignore it." Mr. Marion had spoken the last words slowly, then snapped back to reality. "We're still prayin' for the boy, but the doctors don't give us much hope," he said as he walked back to the counter.

My God! That was Andy! This was Andy's house! This was Andy's dad! Could things have gotten ANY weirder?!

Suddenly, the note in my purse felt like a ten-pound brick.

All the strange things that had happened to me—all the connections I had sensed—were suddenly coming together. I had only an indistinct picture of what was going on, but I also had an idea about how I could clear it up.

"Is Andrew in a hospital near town?" The old man looked confused by my question but answered.

"Yeah, couple miles up the road."

"What's it called?" I asked.

He still seemed suspicious of me, but he opened a drawer behind the counter and pulled out a map. Walking around the counter, he handed it to me and said, "Chattanooga Medical Hospital. Like I said, not too far."

"Thank you so much, sir," I said sincerely. He nodded at me and turned to make his way upstairs.

I twisted the golden knob in front of me and opened the door, but before I stepped outside, I turned back. "Um, sir?" I called.

He was halfway up the stairs and stopped to look down.

"There was a reason this happened to you son. Don't think the accident was a punishment—for you or him."

The old man seemed shocked by my words, and to tell the truth, I was, too. But after a moment, he actually smiled. With his face brighter, he went back upstairs to his lunch. I could smell it all the way from the door.

Outside, it was sunny and beautiful, a stark contrast to the dark, lonely bookstore. I immediately looked at the map and located the hospital. When I was sure of where I was going, I took off running, but this time, adrenaline kept me from feeling any pain.

Both my mind and my heart raced as fast as my legs. I had an insane gut feeling that I was doing the right thing. For once, I didn't feel like I was lost in a sea of questions and anxiety. I knew what I had to do and I knew how I was going to do it.

Chapter 20

An eerie stillness hung in the air as I made my way up the empty hospital corridor. I could hear the faint echo of my shoes hitting the tiled surface. Time seemed to slow down—for once, not in a hurry to get through the day.

I had asked one of the nurses for Andy's room number, so I found him without a problem.

When I approached the white door, I drew in a deep breath, turned the knob and slowly stepped inside.

The hum of machines and the hushed sound of a television turned down low greeted me as I stepped cautiously into the room. As soon as I saw Andy's limp body lying helplessly in the hospital bed, fresh tears filled my tired eyes.

I hadn't forgiven myself for putting him there in the first place, and seeing him hooked up to all that heavy medical machinery was a slap in the face. I found a chair in a corner of the room and pulled it next to Andy's bed. I sat there for a while, crying quietly and listening to the repetitive heart monitor beeping away. Once my tears finally dried up, I cleared my throat and spoke.

"Um, hi, Andy. Long time no see," I said, not believing how stupid I sounded. I took his still hand in mine and tried again: "Listen, I'm so sorry for what I did to you. The only way I can explain is to say that I'm not… normal. I– I sort of… have these… powers. But I think of them more like a curse." I drew in a deep breath before I continued. "This is going to sound ridiculous, but here goes: I have superhuman strength and speed. I can run at, like, two hundred miles an hour, and I can lift cars and trees and houses. I guess I'm sort of a freakish girl superhero. You might think it sounds cool, but it's definitely not. If I don't restrain my emotions, my powers can be deadly, which explains why you're here. The truth is, my powers might be useful, but I don't really know how to control them."

I felt more tears trickling down my tired face as I tried to continue.

"If I could have, I would have stopped myself when I got mad at you. I want you to know that I'm not a cold-blooded killer. Even though my powers can be dangerous, I've changed. I'm not the monster I used to be. I've discovered that I can control myself a lot better than I thought I could, that I can be around Normals, that I'm not that different from them. I'm just sorry that I had to learn all that by hurting you. I'm truly and utterly sorry, Andy." I buried my face in the blanket on the bed and wept quietly. I had known that it would be difficult to visit Andy, but I hadn't expected that I'd break down.

"Geez, now you're gonna make me cry!"

Did I just hear that voice speaking… *out loud*?

"Yes."

Slowly, I turned in the direction of the familiar voice and sucked in a harsh breath. When I saw who was behind me, I almost fainted. It was impossible!

"You're, you're…" I stuttered.

He laughed a little and gave me an almost blindingly perfect smile.

"Nice to see you, too," he said sarcastically.

His image was like an angel's—literally. He was surrounded by a golden aura, and his baby blue eyes were even brighter than I remembered. He was wearing regular clothes—jeans, sneakers, and a white T-shirt.

I was too stunned to speak. You might think that with my powers and my visions and everything else that had happened over the past three months, I wouldn't be shocked by anything. But right in front of me now was an angel. I couldn't do anything but stare at his perfect image, smiling warmly at me.

"I can see you're confused," he said gently as he took a few steps forward.

"Well, yeah," I said, raising my eyebrows.

He chuckled softly and brushed back some of his sandy blonde hair. "I know, it's a lot to take in, but you can figure it out." Given that my brain refused to process what I was seeing, I wasn't sure he was right. He took a step closer to me. "Go on, think, Alexis," he encouraged.

I nodded and closed my eyes. I bit my lip as I tried to concentrate on the facts that I knew and everything that had happened today.

The information was there—I could sense it—but I couldn't pull it out and put it together.

"I, I can't," I said tensely, feeling frustrated.

Suddenly, I felt his strong hand rest lightly on my shoulder. The moment we made contact, everything in my head went into overdrive. My confusion disintegrated, leaving behind only the thoughts that I needed to figure out what was going on.

After a few seconds, my eyes flashed open and I saw him smiling at me.

"Oh my gosh… Andy, it's really you." He nodded lightly as he took his hand off my shoulder.

"Do you understand now?" he asked pleasantly.

"Most of it… yeah," I said, a touch of pride in my voice and a smile on my face.

"But?" he asked.

My smile disappeared, and I looked at him with dismay. "But there's more to figure out."

"That's right."

"You're still in a coma, aren't you?" I reluctantly asked as I looked over my shoulder at Andy's physical body, which was still lying in bed.

He closed his eyes and nodded. "I am human, after all." I looked at him with disbelief, and he laughed at my reaction. "Well, obviously, not now, but I am when I'm in my body. Even if I do have weird powers," he said, chuckling to himself.

"That's how you knew about me and my mom?"

"Yes, like I said in the note, Alexis, you're not alone." There was a moment of silence before Andy spoke again.

"You see, Alexis, starting from the day I was born," he paused as he turned away from me, "I had the power of foreknowledge."

"You mean like, seeing the future?" I asked.

"Sort of," he began, sitting on the edge of his own bed while I remained pinned to my chair (thinking, *Oh yeah, I'll just sit here and chat with the angel*). "I couldn't really *see* the future in visions or anything. It was more of a feeling… like instinct. I can't really describe it. I just always knew things."

He paused, collecting himself before he continued.

"So from the day I was born, I knew my fate," he said darkly.

"You knew this was going to happen?" I asked, fascinated by his words.

"Yes, and I knew how and when." The air was silent between us before I finally pieced together what he was saying.

"You knew this had to happen to get me to where I am now," I breathed to myself. Andy heard me and looked up. "You knew that the end of your life—well, sort of the end—would finally be the beginning for mine," I continued.

Andy turned toward me and smiled. "Good, keep going."

"You sacrificed yourself… for me," I said, feeling love for Andy suddenly swell in my heart and a smile spread across my face.

"Not only for you but for people everywhere," he said distantly.

"What?" I asked, shocked.

"I'm sorry, I'm saying too much."

I nodded and thought for a moment. "But everything that's happened to me—is it connected?" I asked.

"Yes, everything is part of a great plan."

"I don't suppose you can tell me what that is?" I asked sarcastically.

"Nope," he said, making a face at me. I tried to hit him, but he dodged my punch.

I was suddenly taken by how easily this conversation was going. I mean, I was sitting with a guy I had nearly killed three months ago... and we were acting like best friends. It almost seemed like the accident had never happened and we had finally become the friends we couldn't be when Andy was alive.

Well, technically, he was still alive... but you get the point.

Plus, finding out that he *knew* I was going to hurt him all along but still went out of his way to meet me and try to warn me was amazing. *He* was amazing.

"Are you, like, my guardian angel now?" I asked with a half smile.

He laughed and said, "Yeah, I guess we can call it that." As our conversation continued, I thought of more and more questions.

"You're the voice in my head?" I asked.

"Yes, that's me," he confirmed. "I can't tell you how hard it is to get my thoughts into yours... your mind is just one big black fog," he said, frustrated.

"So I've been told," I replied irritably. "Can you tell me why I have that in my head or what it is?"

"No, the most I can tell you is what I wrote in that note," he said. "Please don't lose that. It will help you greatly in the future."

"I'll keep it safe," I promised. He smiled at me again and turned his gaze away, focusing on something else. A few minutes passed before I spoke again.

"You know, there's a lot I don't know about myself. I used to not care where I got my powers from or how they worked. I used to think that I was a threat to everyone who came into contact to me. But lately, everything has changed. I don't know what to do anymore," I said as I played with the hem of my tattered skirt.

Andy drew in a breath and said, "Did you ever think that, maybe, instead of ignoring your powers, you should try to understand them?"

I thought for a long moment before Andy spoke again.

"But you don't have to do it alone. I can help you; you just need to ask the right questions."

"How do I know what questions are the right ones to ask?"

"When I can answer them."

Another long, quiet moment passed before I asked, "So, understanding my powers. Does that mean I need to... *practice*?"

Andy smiled and said, "Now that was a good question. Yes. To completely understand something, you need to have mastery over it. You need to learn everything you can about your powers—how fast and how strong you really are, how you can turn your strength on and off, even where your powers came from."

I nodded and smiled as I looked into his bright eyes.

Finally! I could get some *clear* answers! I could actually learn something about myself—other than the fact I'm a freak of nature.

I looked down at the white floor as my smile disintegrated.

"When do you have to leave?" I asked hesitantly.

He breathed out slowly and said, "To tell you the truth, I really shouldn't even be here right now."

"You have to go soon?" I asked, saddened by the thought.

"Physically, yes. But I'll always be with you in spirit. There's no escaping me!" he said with a playful smile. I laughed along with him.

"Yeah, I probably need to get home, too."

"That's a good idea," he said as he stood. He offered his hand, and I took it as I rose from the chair.

"But one more thing," I said. He looked at me in confusion. "Why are you so nice now? When you were at school, you were a total pain in my butt!" I said, half joking and half dead serious.

He laughed again and answered, "Sadly, it was the only way to get you angry enough to come after me."

Somehow, that made sense.

"I'm so proud of the improvement you've made, Alexis," Andy said, smiling at me with admiration. I blushed a little as he continued. "You've matured a lot in these past three months. You're taking charge of your own destiny, and you've conquered one of your biggest fears—you've finally learned to trust yourself enough to be around other people."

"Well, I *am* one of them, after all." I couldn't believe I was saying it, but I realized that it was true. "I'm just… special."

His grin grew even bigger as I spoke. But after a moment, it disappeared.

"You're still afraid though." My head dropped and my gaze met the floor. I knew what he was talking about. "Don't be. Letting new people into your life can be a good thing," he said. I nodded weakly in response.

Andy stepped closer and pulled me to him. "Don't ever feel like you're alone; I'm always going to be around to help you, I promise," he said, breathing into my hair. We hugged for a long moment, until he slowly released me.

Feeling tears spring into my eyes, I said, "Thank you. For everything."

He reached out and smoothed my tangled hair. "Until next time, my warrior." With those words, Andy's image disintegrated in a shimmer of brilliant gold, and he was gone.

Now it was just me and his unconscious body, with new knowledge, new questions, and a new start.

BZZZZZZ! BZZZZZZZ!

Reaching into my purse, I answered.

"Hi, Mom, I'm on my way home."

Chapter 21

"I was gone for a day?" I asked, trying not to sound too surprised. My mom handed me another soda as Doc continued to clean up my cuts.

"Yes, I called the school and told them you were sick," she said, sitting down next to me on the beige couch and smoothing my damp, clean hair. "We're just so glad that you're safe."

I smiled and said, "More than that, I'm... better, happier! I've finally found some answers." My mom smiled, as well. She was amazed by my story about my trip to Tennessee. I'm not sure she believed me at first, but then she noticed the change in me and realized I was telling the truth.

"Yeah, I finally accepted the fact that I belong with other people. There's no doubt now," I said with confidence.

"Well, you know—" Doc's sentence was cut short when his daughter, Ella, bounced into the room.

Her light brown hair framed her pale little face, and her pink skirt swirled around her as she danced into the room like a ballerina.

She jumped in between my mom and me on the sofa and began squeaking happily about her new stuffed animal.

She was a funny little munchkin.

Speaking of munchkins, Doc's other daughter, Amy, also joined us in the living room. With her shoulder-length brown hair and deep brown eyes, she looked much more grown up and serious than her little sister.

"'S'up munchkins?" I asked the girls.

Ella giggled and hid herself in a blanket while Amy answered, "Nothing much. What happened?" she asked, looking at my arm nervously.

"I… fell at my friend's house. A stick cut me," I said lamely.

"Oh, that's where you were today? I thought you were at school."

Unfortunately, Amy wasn't as easy to fool as Ella. Amy had always known that there was something off about me. I'd planned to tell her about my powers eventually, but now wasn't the right time.

"She stayed home today because she didn't feel good, but she went over to her friend's house to get her homework. Then she slipped walking back to the car," my mother said, making up for my stupid excuse.

"Ouch," Amy said, still not sounding too convinced.

"There you are, good to go," Doc said, as he finished wrapping my arm.

"Thanks," I replied.

"Alexis, can I draw on your band-aid?" Ella asked.

I laughed and said, "Sure kiddo." She giggled happily and went off to find her markers.

"You must have slipped pretty bad at your friend's house," Amy said.

"Uh, not too bad," I replied.

"Then why do you already have huge bruises showing up?" she asked suspiciously.

"I'm… an easy bruiser," I said nervously.

"Then why—"

"Amy, go gather up your schoolwork; we'll be going home soon," Doc interrupted before she could finish her sentence.

"Okay," she said, making her way slowly upstairs.

Man, that was one smart kid.

When Amy was out of sight, my mom turned to me and asked, "When are we going to tell her?"

"What do you mean 'when'?" Doc asked. "Why do you need to tell her?"

"You saw what just happened, Kent. She's going to piece it together sooner or later," my mother said.

"I don't know," I replied, answering my mother's question. "I think when the time is right, I'll know. But I want her to hear it from me."

My mom frowned at me, but Doc said, "It's your secret; you can tell whoever you want whenever you're ready."

I nodded and smiled at him.

"I better go see where Ella went," he said as he collected the first aid stuff and walked out of the room.

I was about to get up and go to my room, but by mom had me by the arm and motioned me to sit back down.

"What's up?" I asked nervously, wondering why she looked so serious all of a sudden.

"I need to talk to you about something, but I don't really know how to start," she said.

"You want me to tell you what I think of you and Doc officially dating," I said, finishing her thought for her.

She looked up, surprised by my words. "Yes, how did you…"

"Mom, I'm not blind," I joked. She laughed nervously. "If he makes you happy, then why not? It's going to take some getting used to on my part, but I think it's a good idea." Despite my cheerful little speech, I could feel my throat closing up on me a little bit.

My mom smiled and gave me a hug. "I think, in the long run, it's going to make things better."

I nodded as I let go of her and stood up from the couch. "I'm going to take a nap. I'm still exhausted from my trip."

She nodded happily and allowed me to go to my room. As I reached the top of the stairs, I met Amy, with a worried expression on her face.

She had been sitting on the top step the entire time Mom, Doc, and I had been talking in the living room. Did she hear our conversation about my powers? Judging from her confused stare, I guessed that she did.

"Look, Amy— " I began, but she cut me off.

"I like you a lot, Lex," she said shyly, "but I wish you wouldn't keep a secret from me. My teacher said that secrets are bad."

Wow, this kid could really pull at your heart. I took a deep breath and replied, "I like you a lot, too, Amy. And your teacher's right; secrets can hurt people. But sometimes, kids have to be a little more grown up before they can understand secrets. I promise that when the time is right, I'll tell you every secret there is to know about me. Okay?"

I could tell she wasn't happy with my answer, but she nodded in agreement. I gave her a tired smile, then opened my bedroom door and stepped inside.

As soon as the door was closed, I collapsed on my bed, still feeling sad about Andy, confused about Mom and Doc, and a little guilty about not being honest with Amy. I felt tears of exhaustion begin to leak out of my eyes

"*Change is difficult, but that doesn't mean it's bad.*" Hearing Andy's voice made me feel a little better. I hugged my pillow and finally fell asleep.

ꝏ

"There you are!" Mandy exclaimed when she saw me. I smiled at her and waved.

"Where were you yesterday?" Sophia asked, poking her head out from behind her locker door.

"I didn't feel good, so I stayed home," I replied casually as I twirled the combination dial on my locker. After I had it open, I glanced over at Ariella, who was staring at my arm with confusion.

"I ran into a nail that was sticking out of a wall," I said, looking at the bandage on my arm.

"Did you draw all those hearts on there?" Mandy laughed, looking at the bandage as well.

"Ha-ha, no, my stepsister did."

"Aw that's cute," Sophia said, smiling.

Being back with my friends at school felt great. I never thought I'd hear myself say that I enjoyed school or that I had Normals for friends, but now I did. Most important, I thought of myself as one of them. I guess I had grown up a lot.

Mandy and Sophia gathered their things and walked off to first period. I moved to follow, but Ariella stopped me.

"What really happened?" she asked.

"What do you mean?" I said, feeling my breath speed up.

"You know what I mean," she said, lifting my hurt arm.

I jerked it away and said, "I told you what happened. What are you implying?"

She looked away for a second and said, "Forget it. It's nothing."

I looked at her skeptically but decided to change the subject. "Hey, my mom said you guys could spend the night over spring break if you want to."

My diversion seemed to work. Ariella's face lit up, and she immediately started making plans. Then, her eyes abruptly hardened and she stopped speaking in the middle of a sentence. She was glaring at someone behind me, her arms crossed in front of her chest.

I turned slowly around and saw Taylor.

"Sorry for interrupting," he said, looking at Ariella. She rolled her eyes at him as he turned his gaze back to me. "Can we talk?"

I looked at him with an expressionless face. Inside, I was an emotional hurricane, but outside, I tried to remain stoic.

"I guess," I said in a bored voice. I looked over at Ariella, who raised her eyebrows in a look that said, "Let him have it" and sauntered away.

No one had to tell me that twice.

I turned back to Taylor, once again looking into his dark, unreadable eyes.

"What do you want?" I demanded.

"A chance to explain?" he offered.

"What's there to explain? Everything seems clear to me," I replied.

I was pretty proud of how well I was holding up. I was as cold and hard as a stone. No way would I let him have the pleasure of knowing that he had hurt me. I had to fight back tears, but in the back of my mind, I promised myself a meltdown later at home.

Taylor opened his mouth to speak, but the warning bell interrupted before he could say anything.

"Well, this was fun," I said sarcastically and turned to walk away.

"Alexis, wait." He grabbed my good arm to hold me back. I turned toward him, my eyes beginning to burn and my jaw clenched. Did he really just do that?

"Let go," I said with a deadly voice. He let out a short, impatient breath and continued to stare intensely into my eyes.

"Look," he said with an edge in his voice, "I'm not going to drop this. You might as well deal with it now, or I'll just keep coming back." I kept quiet as he continued. "If you want me to go away, then you'll have to tell me. Tell me to leave you alone," he taunted. I didn't say anything. His eyes softened a little, and he released my arm.

"About a mile up the road, there's a forest. Meet me there after school." With that, he turned and disappeared around the corner, leaving me alone in the silence and stillness of the concrete hallway.

I gripped my textbook, trying to restrain my shaking body from running away, and bit my lip to keep myself from crying.

Just when I was getting along so well, why did he have to come along and confuse me?

Chapter 22

The idea of meeting Taylor in the forest had kicked my mind into panic mode. Everything around me seemed surreal. I was so anxious and wired that just one little twitch from the wrong person would be enough to make me explode.

"What are you going to say?" Ariella asked as I nervously put my books away.

All day, I had thought about nothing else. But I had a feeling that when the time came, I would be too weak to say anything. Sometimes I'm pathetic like that.

"I don't know," I said, feeling my stomach drop.

"What do you think *he's* going to say?"

Half grinning, I managed to say, "Probably something stupid."

She laughed and I couldn't help but laugh, too, momentarily suppressing my worry.

But trepidation quickly flooded back into my veins. I said, "I don't know; I'm kind of planning on not going."

Ariella thought for a moment, leaning against her locker, then spoke: "I think you should go." I looked at her with astonishment.

"Um, were you not sober when I told you about what he did?" I asked sourly.

"Kissing May when he says he likes you was messed up…" she paused, as if questioning herself for a moment, then continued. "But I don't think you should let some little thing stand between you and him being together."

"I'm not sure May is 'some little thing,'" I mumbled.

She looked at me warily but didn't bother to ask what I was grumbling about.

I finally stood up on my shaky legs and hung my backpack over my trembling shoulder.

"Besides," I said, "I think it's going to rain soon."

Ariella gave me a disapproving look and laughed. "You're really going to let a little rain bother you?"

"Hey, the humidity could ruin my hair!" I replied sarcastically.

She scoffed and playfully punched me in the arm.

"I'm serious," she said, no longer sounding as if she was teasing. "If you don't go, I think you'll really regret it."

I looked down as a wave of freshly electrified nerves washed over me. I was having second thoughts—actually, more like twentieth thoughts.

What would happen if I met Taylor in the forest? Would my dream about shattering him come true? And even if it didn't, what would we say to each other? If I went, would that mean that I was saying yes to him? On the other hand, what if I *didn't* go? Would he take that as a definite no? Because I wasn't even sure if I was saying no or not.

The bottom line was that I had no clue how this meeting would go down… which scared the crap out of me.

"*Take what you know and let go of the unknown. Stop living in fear.*"

Andy was right… as usual. I was going to have to deal with Taylor eventually; might as well get it over with.

"*Not exactly what I meant…*," Andy said critically.

Taking in a shallow breath, I mentally brushed him off as I said goodbye to Ariella.

"Call me later, okay?" I nodded in response and turned to walk away.

"*The only thing keeping you away from him is you*," Andy pushed. "*Forget your 'shattering' dream; I told you, you don't have to fear your powers.*"

I cringed with every word he spoke. It was all true, no doubt about that… but it was much easier said than done.

With Andy's voice still ringing in my ears and disturbing images flashing in my head, I made my way to the woods behind the school—a shortcut to get to the meeting place—where I would run, head on, *toward* my fear that I was destined to kill Taylor.

I really hoped I had misinterpreted that dream.

☙

It only took me a few seconds to arrive at Taylor's meeting spot, but already the rain had seeped through my clothes. (Thank goodness I wasn't wearing a white shirt.)

The rain was heavier out in the open than it was underneath the tall trees, but even with their branches acting as an umbrella, I was still miserably wet. The forest was alive with a soft symphony of buzzing insects and screeching tree frogs. The air was thick and muggy, but I could still make out the slight freshness brought by the rain, along with the thick scents of soggy bark and wet dirt. The entire woods looked dreary, with no break in the gray clouds above.

Standing in the rain, feeling every drop of water that hit my clammy skin and hearing every rustle of every creature that inhabited these woods, was strangely therapeutic. I felt as if I was listening to the sounds of the rain forest on one of those meditation tapes—the kind that people buy to help them sleep better.

Although I could do without the annoying tree frogs.

Suddenly, the sound of someone walking, rustling damp leaves and breaking small twigs with each step, interrupted my trance.

Of course, under ordinary circumstances, my first instinct would be to throw my fists up and fight whatever was coming toward me. But I knew exactly who it was before he stepped through the trees.

He wandered out of the thick part of the woods, emerging from the dark shadows. He still wore his school uniform, but he had taken off his polo and was wearing a black v-neck undershirt. As he lifted his gaze from the ground, a grin erased his stoic expression, and his eyes seemed to light up.

"You came," Taylor said, sounding pleasantly surprised.

"Yeah, yeah," I said, trying to seem uninterested, even though just hearing his smooth voice caused my heart to flutter eagerly.

He continued walking forward, his eyes fixed on me, as I tried to focus on my breathing—and not on how amazing he looked.

His shirt clung to his body, outlining his perfect chest. The rain had made his hair look longer and darker. His face, too, was different.

Normally, his expression seemed more reserved. Sometimes, he almost looked dangerous. But now, he was open, as if a door had been unlocked to a different Taylor, one I had never known before and never expected to meet.

"Well?" I asked tensely, trying to keep my mind on how angry I was at him (without losing my temper, of course).

He cleared his throat nervously and began, "Um, yeah. Listen..."

"I'm listening," I said, purposely interrupting him. He shot me a look but ignored my remark and kept talking.

"That whole thing with May—that was just..."

"What whole thing with May?" I asked mockingly. He was getting angry now. I could see his eyes hardening again and his features growing stiffer.

"Look, Alexis," he restarted with clenched teeth. "I'm trying to apologize. You're not making this easy."

"Oh, I'm sorry. I certainly wouldn't want to make anything difficult for you!" I fired back sourly.

"What's your problem?" he asked.

"You don't get it, do you?!" I shouted. "You have NO idea what I've been through these past three months! My life has been one brutal battle after another—especially with you! You just don't realize what you're getting yourself into." I paused, taking a breath before I continued with my tirade. "I'm sorry if I'm being a little difficult. I'm sorry that I've been trying my best to keep you safe by staying away from you. OH! And I am *SO* SORRY that I love you!"

As I finished, everything around me seemed to come to a dead halt; even the tree frogs went silent.

"*At last*," Andy said with exaggerated relief.

I looked up with a burning face to see Taylor, *smiling*. Before I could wrap my mind around what I had just said, he was holding my face gently between his hands. As he moved his face toward mine, I could feel my heart crash into my rib cage and my stomach drop. His lips had barely touched my quivering mouth when I broke free of his hold and jumped back.

He looked at me with questioning eyes and a perplexed expression.

"We… I … can't do this," I said, stammering.

"What do you mean?"

I couldn't let this go any farther. I had to stop now, before I lost the ability to stop. I had to do something to make him change his mind, make him leave—heck!—make him run away screaming!

Panicking, I wrapped my arms around a tree trunk that stood next to me, making sure I had a good hold.

"*No, Alexis! You don't have to do this!*" Andy warned.

"This is the only way," I said out loud. "It's the only way to be safe."

With that, I uprooted the thirty-foot-tall oak tree with ease, holding it horizontally over my head.

Taylor's eyes grew huge when he saw my strength. He stumbled back a few feet in surprise and almost landed on his butt.

I felt torn. I didn't want him to go—I wanted him to stay with me—but I knew that driving him away was the only way to keep him safe. I couldn't risk hurting him.

"*How can I get this through your thick skull?*" Andy asked, sounding nothing like the angel I had met in the hospital. "*He loves you. You love him. You have more control than you think you do! Stop living in fear.*"

Suddenly, as if someone had flipped a switch in my brain to the "on" position, Andy's meaning became crystal clear.

I wasn't angry now—not in the least. If I were, Taylor would be dead by now. I was in complete control of my powers.

By trying to protect Taylor, I was hurting him—and myself. The truth was that we loved each other and wanted desperately to be together.

Everything that had happened to me—everything that I'd thought of as a punishment—had happened for a reason: to bring me to Taylor.

I dropped the oak tree next to me, feeling the tremble of the ground under my feet. I sat on the fallen log and allowed my head to fall into my hands. The tears came without my permission.

My life sucked. I had been living in a state of fear—about my powers, about Taylor, about my dreams—and by the time I finally saw the truth, I ruined the one chance I had to be happy.

I lifted my face to see if Taylor had taken off running, but a flash of light caught my eye. Looking down at a small puddle of water, I saw my reflection. Staring back at me were my burning white eyes and my tear—and rain—streaked face.

Great, like scaring him to death with the tree wasn't enough.

I heard marshy steps coming toward me, but I turned my face away; I didn't want Taylor to see my eyes.

He sat down on the tree next to me, looking off into the forest. After a long, quiet moment, he turned and took one of my hands in his. With his free hand, he delicately cupped my chin, turning my head to look straight into his eyes.

My eyes were so intensely bright that I could actually see them staring back at me in Taylor's gaze.

I sighed as I allowed him to stare. He looked slightly stunned, but he quickly shook it away as he leaned in a little closer.

"You're gonna have to do a lot worse than *that* to get rid of me," he said, wearing the lopsided grin that I loved.

I returned the smile as he continued to admire my eyes.

He was perfect for me. I couldn't explain it… I just felt it. Which I guess is what love is all about. I felt like we were meant to be together.

Suddenly, his lips were on mine, short-circuiting the last thought left in my mind.

It sounds goofy to say it, but his kiss was everything I had dreamed of… and more. He wrapped his arms around me, and I could feel the heat of his body seeping through my soaked clothes. Being this close to him, *kissing* him! It was just amazing!

Suddenly, everything that had happened in these last few months—starting from the day I met Taylor—somehow seemed to make sense, to have a purpose. Being with him here and now… well, I think I would go through it all again, just so I could arrive in this same place.

It's what Andy had been telling me all along. Letting go of my fear brought me to a better place, a happier place. Although my powers—along with many other things—remained a mystery, I was finally on the right path to figuring them out.

"*There will be more challenges, but you have taken the first of many steps: You have been enlightened.*"

Acknowledgements

"I'd like to thank so many people for making this possible. First of all, my family. Mom for her support, Dad for his love, Patti for her encouragement, and Travis for his comic relief—because Lord knows we all need it! I'm so blessed to have you all in my life. Also, to the very first readers of Enlightened: Grandma, Aunt Ann, and Aunt Peg. Thank you for believing in me…and Alexis! Debby Nolan, my super-editor, for her help, advice, and her always gentle ways. (Oh, and her sarcasm, too!) Thank you to all of my amazing friends for being there for me through thick and thin! Also, my three beautiful little sisters: Kelly, Avery, and Emelie. I love you guys more than you could ever know!

And, just because she begged me to: Sarah Wilhoit.

You're welcome.